MURDER IN THE SHADOWS

A VIOLET CARLYLE HISTORICAL MYSTERY

BETH BYERS

SUMMARY

November 1925

Violet and Victor are called to London by the most unexpected of people--Lady Eleanor. She's in trouble and when the chips are down, she turns for help to the stepdaughter she'd alienated and the stepson she barely tolerates.

Will they find it within themselves to help her? And if so, what will they do with what they find?

CHAPTER 1

"You have a note from Lady Eleanor," Victor said as Violet walked into the breakfast room. Violet scowled towards the pile of letters that had been placed next to her seat. The only thing she wanted was a letter from Jack, but Victor would have told her if it were there. "Oh, and hullo."

"Hullo," she said absentmindedly, then paused to stare at her twin as his unexpected presence sank in. Given that he had his own country house a few short kilometers away, she wasn't quite sure why he was in her breakfast room while she was still crusty-eyed and in a kimono.

Normally she'd have dressed before coming to the breakfast room, but Jack was gone, she hadn't slept well, and she was debating returning to her bed after her cup of coffee ended her headache. Her eyes were burning, and she was almost incapable of speaking, let alone the verbal sparring that she and Victor usually embraced.

They were silent as they assessed each other.

"I assume she wants something," Vi mused, her twin's opening remark finally pushing past the pounding in her head. She ignored the letter to make her way to the sideboard.

"You couldn't sleep either?"

"I'm often sleepless." Vi shook her head. "Why can't you?"

"Kate," was his only reply, referring to his traveling wife. "I've already sent for more coffee."

With matching features, matching history, and a near supernatural bond, their sharp eyes glinted at the same moment as they examined one another. They might not live in the same old rooms anymore, they might both be married now and no longer share everything, but they were still able to communicate with a simple look.

Violet gave her twin a furious look as she poured a scant half-cup of coffee. The nearly-drained carafe made him grimace ruefully, and she staggered back to the breakfast table without enough to counteract her headache.

"I needed that," she told him, pressing her fingers against her forehead.

Victor gave her a woebegone expression that did nothing to soften her.

"I'm a crippled man." He leaned back, pushing away his empty plate, bemoaning his own unhappiness. "I thought, 'I don't want Kate to go, let alone take the twins, but at least I'll be able to sleep through the night and get some work done.' Ridiculous. I'm a mockery of who I used to be."

Violet shook her head for both of them. They had

probably both been awake and pacing at the same time the previous night. Writing in the middle of the night? More like waking cold because she'd become accustomed to the warmth of someone's arm over her back, the chill of loneliness invading her bones. No doubt Victor had suffered the same. They'd both have tried to fix it by wrapping themselves tight in the blankets. Only mere covers didn't warm as well after becoming used to another body, so they'd have lain alone in the darkness, wondering if their spouse was awake. Had Jack slept fine without her? Or was he, too, suffering?

Violet lifted her cup in salute to her brother and drank a large swallow. She had returned to bed after clawing enough story out of her mind to allow sleep. Then she'd woken to the unfeeling dog, Holmes, who'd wanted to go out.

"Any word from Jack?" Victor asked.

Violet shook her head, trying to ignore the nauseous rush of worry that accompanied Victor's question. She had to admit, if only to herself, that she was worried sick.

"Still in Leeds?"

Vi nodded and sipped slowly, savoring the coffee. Leeds. Goodness. Jack was working a case with Hamilton. Something dark was going on, and the higher-ups of Scotland Yard had initially sent another man. That fellow called in a report which caused Ham's exit to Leeds. A mere day after Ham's arrival in Leeds, Jack had been called in. Whatever was happening, it was bad. As much as she loved Jack, she was glad to be far away from the crime. She just wanted Jack and Ham far away from it as well.

She'd been debating, previous to this, wanting Jack to

leave his work. She had come to the conclusion that the change needed to be on her part. She'd drawn back from direct control over her business interests. However, her feelings had drastically changed about Jack's work at the moment. With the constant worry for those she loved. She didn't just want Jack out of these cases, she wanted Ham out too.

"How is Kate?" Violet hadn't bothered with food. All she had needed was coffee and she didn't have nearly enough. The thumping in her head declared she might need a whole pot.

"Her mother is still ill and still doesn't want me around. Kate reports the pack of gremlins disguised as orphans are running amuck while our infant angels continue to do well without me."

Victor's scowl had Violet smirking.

"She is ill," Violet told him without sympathy. "Your pain seems to make my head feel better."

"It's my presence, darling. I'm a balm to the soul." Victor nodded towards the letter from Lady Eleanor with a pointed look.

Better to get it out of the way on an empty stomach. She opened it slowly, read the note, blinked rather rapidly, and read it again.

With a deep frown, Violet handed the letter to her twin. He read it as slowly and then said, "I'll go with you. Shall I meet you back here at noon? We can get the next train to London."

Violet nodded and then rose, ringing the bell for Hargreaves, and then returning to her seat. "We can just open my house," Violet told her brother. "No sense in opening up both houses for the two of us, Hargreaves, and a few servants."

"It'll be odd, won't it? To be in London without Kate, Jack, Lila, and Denny. Whatever will we do with ourselves?"

"It'll be like the old days," Violet told him with a wicked grin. "But with better smelling rooms. We might be able to write four books."

"It won't matter if we're in London or here," Victor replied. "There's no sleeping if Kate and Jack are elsewhere. We're going to continue to be useless ninnies who are weak and broken without their partners. We were stronger when we were younger. Now? Vi darling, we're useless."

"Surely we can beat this," Violet suggested. "I used to sleep—" She paused long enough to consider and then admitted, "Maybe I've always been weak."

His scoff matched her internal one. Sleep for her had always been a hit or miss prospect.

"Well," Violet told him flatly. "We can be grumpy and sleepless together. Cup upon cup of Turkish coffee in the morning, an afternoon dealing with our stepmother, and then cocktails to get the flavor of her out of our mouths. Like the old days, only now we know what we're missing."

"Drinks are going to be required if we have to deal with Stepmother. I suppose I can play with making a new cocktail to give me something to look forward to. I'll call it Insomnia."

"Sounds bitter and dark," Violet told him.

"It'll be bright. Oh! I have an idea."

"About 'Insomnia?'"

"Indeed. Insomnia—an antidote to internal foulness. It should be something sweet."

"I would drink it."

"You'd drink anything I handed you."

"It's true love," she told him. "A soul bond between womb mates."

He rolled his eyes at her. "I bought a divine blackberry cordial made by a little woman with the deepest wrinkles I've ever seen."

"Bring it," she immediately ordered.

"Yes, obviously." Victor shot her a quiet look and then added, "My wrinkled angel and her grandchildren hunt blackberries together. They make the wine using a recipe from her grandmother. Can you imagine? She gave me the recipe and had the wicked gall to charge me a hundred pounds for it."

"She's your angel?"

He grinned, but didn't expand.

Vi shook her head. "You gave her the money because you liked her." Violet knew him too well to need the particulars. "She might make the most divine cordial you've ever had, but you could have gotten a dozen local recipes—nearly as good—for less than a fiver."

"I was buying their love. Especially my angel's love," he told her unrepentantly. "They said I could join the blackberry hunt and make the wine with them for a price. That hundred pounds was, I fear, the down payment. I'm thinking I might need to create my own business. Vi, can you see it? Carlyle Fine Wines & Spirits?"

"Save your pin money if you're basing it off of this

blackberry cordial," Violet advised her twin. "You've fallen in with sharks. And yes, I can see it. I love the idea."

"Good," Victor told her with a grin. "You'll be investing of course. Also, I told my ancient cordial-making love that we're dedicating the next book to her."

Violet laughed. "Shall we poison someone with wine? What do you think she wants?" she added without amusement, knowing they were procrastinating.

"Poison by a sweet cordial is perfect," he answered, but he didn't need the explanation that Violet's mind had returned to their stepmother. He shrugged and then moaned in joy when the coffee arrived. He rose, taking Vi's cup, and refilled both of their glasses only to return to the buffet and make a piece of toast for Violet.

"Eat, darling. You'll need your strength for our stepmother."

"Maybe while we're in London, we can pop over and see Ginny at her new school." Another procrastination technique to delay facing their stepmother, though a pleasant and necessary one.

"Ah, something to look forward to." Victor nodded, a worried look crossing his face. "Even as a father myself, Ginny leaves me helpless. You'd think having her first would make me more confident in Vivi and Agatha, but instead—I'm just afraid of facing the twins when they're older."

Violet had little doubt that he was wondering if they'd allowed Ginny too much freedom in a school that didn't require attendance and allowed the students to select their own courses of study. Ginny was their ward, and they were responsible for her. As adults who weren't prepared for someone as clever and rambunctious as Ginny, they were blind and stupid.

"I want to catch her unawares and see if she's studying to be a doctor or the finer aspects of napping under a tree like you and I would have." Violet wished that Ginny had decided to stay with them instead. Private study, an excellent tutor, their love, support—and most importantly, their ready gazes.

"Can we hold her to task if she is doing what we would have?"

Victor winced. "I think we have to admit to ourselves that we were terrible creatures and want something better for our Ginny. We have to lie to her, Vi. I bet you Father stepped out on his classes more often than we did and for less wholesome reasons. Then he lied to us about it later."

Violet shot her twin a look that ordered him to not speak of Father. It wasn't as if Father had been involved in their education anyway. Not really. Victor's replying glance told Violet she'd have to get over her squabble with Father sooner or later.

Violet's response was to ask, "Have you heard from Isolde or Tomas?"

"Our dear little sister and Tomas have moved from Belgium to Yugoslavia. He says they took some lovely rooms and that the baby is fat and brilliant."

Violet frowned and swirled her coffee. She hadn't gotten to meet Isolde's baby yet as Tomas had whisked her out of the country before the babe had made an entrance.

Vi's mind returned to and escaped from Lady Eleanor with predictable regularity, especially lately. Violet had made a promise to help Lady Eleanor at a future date, but Vi hadn't expected to be called back to London with a note that felt like a cross between an anxious plea for help and a summons from the queen.

Violet finished her coffee, ate the toast under Victor's steely eye, and went to pack her trunks. She had yet to replace her personal maid and was too particular to let any random housemaid rummage through her things. She had one of the housemaids bring a trunk to her room and packed her books first. Once her reading was covered, Violet put her typewriter in its travel case, added plenty of paper, typing ribbon, and the small tool case that went along with the typewriter.

Vi followed the most important things with cosmetics and then faced her closet. Pajamas were obvious. A few kimonos. Her underthings. A snuggly robe. Shoes. Violet considered her closet, starting with day dresses appropriate for winter, evening gowns for when she and Victor inevitably went for cocktails and dancing. Vi added her mink coat and then put together several cloches.

She moved from packing to writing a long letter to Jack before they left, sealed it, and then looked up at the sound of Victor clearing his throat. He was leaning against her bedroom door, watching her as though he knew exactly what she was doing--delaying the journey to London. Violet let him wait, taking the brown leather bag from Jack's closet to put her current book in it, her current manuscript, a fountain pen, her journal, and a small box of chocolates.

"The dogs?" Victor asked. He was in no hurry either,

considering he would have to return to his house to pack.

Violet looked at his feet where his dog, Gin, was leaning against his leg.

"Yes, of course." Violet tossed her brother two leashes and he let out a piercing whistle. Violet shot him a dark look and glanced towards the fireplace where her two dogs, Holmes and Rouge, and their progeny were snuggled on a pillow. The puppies would need to be placed in a basket.

"Maybe we should motor up," Violet said, trying to imagine handling them on the train without a servant. A basketful of puppies on a long train ride up to London sounded disgusting.

"We could," Victor said. "Did Jack leave the feces auto?"

"Jack sold the feces auto and ordered another one. He made it a different color, but the rest is the same. The new auto, however, has yet to arrive. He drove his old one to Leeds."

"We'll take mine then," Victor said. "I just wanted to say feces auto."

"Save it for when Jack is here," Violet told him. "The brat who destroyed his auto is lucky that he didn't strangle her. Her father is lucky that we only billed him for the difference after we sold the first auto, and for the repairs of course."

She and Jack had been the victims of dark pranks. It had ended when Violet realized the perpetrator and cornered the girl's parents with the help of Lady Eleanor. The price for Lady Eleanor's help was a favor that was now being called in.

CHAPTER 2

"*M*rs. Vi?" Hargreaves asked two days later. London was drizzly and grey with clouds that carpeted the sky and a chill that reached into Vi's bones. It was cold at the country house too, but somehow it seemed cozier.

Violet looked up from her manuscript and the notes Victor had left. She was sitting on the olive green Chesterfield, her feet propped in front of her on the sofa. Next to her, a tray held a cup of Turkish coffee, an ignored scone, and the remnants of a raspberry and chocolate tart. Vi's feet were warmed by her dog, Holmes. Rouge and the puppies were in the kitchen being spoiled by Hargreaves and the rest of the servants, but Violet had sought and received a good snuggle earlier that day.

"Lady Eleanor has arrived."

Violet didn't even try to hide her sigh as she ordered tea, more coffee and her twin to the parlor. She slowly sat up, setting aside her manuscript, rubbed Holmes's belly, and waited for Victor. It was a well-established practice to face their stepmother united.

Violet took a seat near the fire and pointed her toes towards the flames. Breathe, she told herself. Breathe and think terrible thoughts. Auto accidents. Bad fish. A trip down the stairs. A wrenched knee. None of it would be enough, Violet thought, for the endless sourness to come.

Victor silently took the seat next to Violet just ahead of Lady Eleanor's arrival. The twins turned, as one, towards their stepmother. Violet took in Lady Eleanor's expensive day dress, perfectly matching shoes and clutch, a cameo broach on her chest, and expensive earbobs on her ears. She was wearing a small hat on the back of her head and had a strand of pearls around her neck.

It wasn't the richness of Lady Eleanor's attire that caught Violet's attention but the low-level flush that didn't fade despite settling herself comfortably. Vi considered her stepmother's blush as she watched the woman uncompromisingly. Lady Eleanor had tried to rule over the twins for the entirety of their lives. Seeing Lady Eleanor discombobulated in their presence was a huge insight into the nature of what was happening with her. She didn't quite meet the twins' eyes. Another huge sign that the situation truly was terribly wrong.

Violet was surprised by the flash of concern. She had been coming to the realization that there was a level of kindness in Lady Eleanor when she nudged the twins towards Aunt Agatha. Was it wrong to not love your stepchildren if you recognized you couldn't and helped your partner hand them to someone who would? Maybe, but Violet had to think that she was better for the honesty. She wasn't sure, however, that she could credit Lady Eleanor with that level of self-awareness. Perhaps the fact that Aunt Agatha was everything the twins needed was simply a lucky by-product.

That was all besides the current point, however. Something was happening in Lady Eleanor's mind that made it hard for her to keep still. Perhaps why Lady Eleanor immediately tried to put Vi and Victor on the defensive. It wasn't going to work.

"What are you doing here?" Lady Eleanor asked, scowling at Victor before her mean gaze fell on Violet. "Still as slim as ever. Are you barren or have you and Jack had a falling out?" Her attempt wasn't going to work. Things like that hadn't worked in years and all three of them knew it.

Violet glanced at her brother in order to cleanse her visual palette. His grey pinstriped suit was accented by a bright yellow shirt. He'd finished it with a black and grey paisley tie and shining shoes. He looked like a spoiled, useless man. She supposed it was mean, but every time she saw him so shiny she thought of how the number of men who'd inherited enough to be lazy were dwindling.

"Is there a reason you're starting out vile?" Victor's gaze shot to Violet. "I understand you need Vi's help."

Lady Eleanor's mouth tightened and then she said, "Always united. Even married. You two are here together instead of where God intended you to be."

"If you mean hunting murderers with Jack in Leeds?" Violet asked calmly.

Lady Eleanor's gaze narrowed darkly at the reference to Jack's career.

"Or attending to the sickbed of my mother-in-law?" Victor added helpfully.

Lady Eleanor closed her eyes and breathed slowly in. She struggled for composure, which was so typical of the woman. She went on the attack and then was offended when the twins united.

"Where are all your hangers-on? I'm surprised there isn't a snarky and unwelcome audience."

Violet was not a delicate flower despite her name, so she wasn't gentle. "Are you referring to the family we created for ourselves? Because if so, Lila and Denny are in Paris. Rita is in Scotland with her father. Kate is taking care of her mother. The twins and nanny are with her. Jack is assisting Ham in Leeds. Isolde and Tomas"— Violet took mean and wicked delight in Lady Eleanor's dark look—"are in Yugoslavia, and Ginny is at school. There are, of course, others we love, but you inferred that time was of the essence when you summarily summoned us to London. Perhaps you'd like to get on with what you need."

The replacement family that they'd created, after their own had been unsatisfactory, didn't bother Lady Eleanor in the slightest.

"What do you want, Lady Eleanor?" Victor's feelings were clear. Violet had heard them in detail as they motored up. Lady Eleanor helped Violet trap the evil brat of a prankster, an act that should have been done because they were family. Instead, Violet was going to be harassed into dealing with a matter that Lady Eleanor didn't want to do. Would it have been too much to just help Violet when she needed it?

Lady Eleanor blushed brightly, licking her lips. She

glanced between them, pausing when the teacart arrived. Violet poured her a cup of tea, handed her a plate of sandwiches and biscuits and then glanced at Victor. He'd poured his own coffee while Violet was playing hostess and had already finished all of the liver pâté sandwiches that he'd loaded onto his plate.

Vi poured her own coffee and ignored the food. Despite the comfort of tea and food, Lady Eleanor's ruddiness didn't fade.

"I helped you. You're supposed to help me. That was our agreement."

"I promised you a favor when you helped me around All Hallows. It is a promise I will keep. May we get on with it?"

She considered prodding her stepmother further but decided to wait. Violet drank her cup of coffee while her stepmother said nothing at all. Victor followed Violet's lead and they sat in awkward silence for far too long.

"I assume I can count on your discretion?"

Violet nibbled on her bottom lip as she considered. Finally, Violet said, "As long as my morals aren't compromised, I will keep your secrets from everyone but Jack."

"Who do you think I am?" Lady Eleanor demanded, her gaze enraged. "Morals compromised? What madness is this that you would dare to speak to me this way?" She was winding herself up. "I am your stepmother! Have you forgotten?"

"If only we could," Victor muttered.

"I think you are taking a rather long time to get to the point," Violet answered her stepmother, "which raises some distinct concerns. We have conflicting points of view about certain subjects, and quite frankly," Violet told Lady Eleanor with clear precision, "I don't like you very much."

Lady Eleanor's mouth dropped. "How dare you speak to me this way?"

Before Lady Eleanor could snap another reply, Vi added, "I know the sentiment is returned, and I appreciate that if nothing else, we can at least acknowledge the truth. Victor and I were horrible children, grieving and lost, and you weren't what we needed."

"That wasn't my fault!"

"Agreed," Violet told her, "but it doesn't change that there are rivers and oceans of ill feelings and history behind us. Even still, we are family. If you need help, Victor and I will do what we can for you and employ all of our friends and skills. We'd have done it even if you hadn't helped me with my All Hallows problem."

Lady Eleanor met Violet's gaze. They stared at each other for too long, but unlike with Victor or even Jack, Violet had no idea what was going on inside of her stepmother's head. The woman could be thinking that Violet had ruined her life marrying Jack. Lady Eleanor could be thinking that Violet looked quite ill in her mustard dress and brown jumper. Perhaps she was thinking about a future appointment with a friend. Anything at all could be happening behind that gaze and for once in her life, Violet gave Lady Eleanor the credit that it probably had nothing to do with Violet.

Or perhaps, Violet thought, she'd simply finally grown up enough to realize that everything wasn't about her. Lady Eleanor was the protagonist of her own story, and she was experiencing trauma entirely unrelated to Violet.

Lady Eleanor sniffed deeply and turned her gaze resolutely to the floor. A moment later her story began.

"When Mr. Danvers offered for Isolde, I won't pretend that I didn't think she could do better. Obviously she could. She did end up wed to Tomas. Handsome, rich as Croesus, kind." Better than the overweight, too-old, criminal fiancé Lady Eleanor had pressured Isolde to accept. Luckily for Isolde, and unlucky for Danvers, he was murdered before the wedding could go through.

"Young," Victor added.

"In love with her," Violet added.

"She loves him as well. She's not resigned to him." Victor's tone made Lady Eleanor scowl.

Violet bit down on her lip and fiddled with her wedding ring, thinking back to those early days. Her half-sister, Isolde Carlyle, daughter of an earl, had ended up engaged to the supposedly rich Mr. Danvers. Isolde was lovely, barely eighteen, well connected, and well off in her own right. Everything about the engagement had enraged Violet, especially when Isolde revealed she didn't really want to marry Mr. Danvers.

Even still, Violet had appeared at Kennington House to support the wedding. She'd tried to convince Isolde to back out before it was too late. Vi had, in fact, succeeded, left her sister to change back into a normal dress, and gone for their father. Only, Violet had discovered the dead body of Carlton Danvers before she'd found their father.

Lady Eleanor turned her gaze from the floor to the twins. "Yes, yes. I encouraged Isolde to marry Mr. Danvers. It wasn't like I knew he was a fraud. He was too old for her and she could do better, but as far as I knew, he wasn't..."

"What he was?" Violet asked. She wasn't trying to be cruel, but Lady Eleanor winced.

"You knew he was a villain," Victor shot back without any sympathy.

"Yes, I knew he was a villain." Lady Eleanor closed her eyes. "You have to understand. I love my children. I do. They are my everything, but—"

An actual tear rolled down Lady Eleanor's face and Violet turned to her brother, just slightly lifting a brow. Vi wasn't sure how much she believed the tear. She could tell Victor didn't believe it at all. They waited as Lady Eleanor struggled, Victor handing over his handkerchief perfunctorily.

"If I had to choose between them," Lady Eleanor finally said, "you know I would choose Geoffrey. I wanted the best for Isolde. I did—"

"Nothing about marrying Isolde off to the old, fat, villainous Carlton Danvers was necessary to protect Geoffrey," Victor snapped.

"That's not quite true," Lady Eleanor snapped in return, "but I won't discuss it. It has nothing to do with what I'm experiencing now."

Violet didn't believe that statement. Lady Eleanor began her story with that bit of information. It certainly applied.

"Obviously, he knew something about you? Something he used to get you to push Isolde into a marriage when she could do better?"

"He did have positives," Lady Eleanor defended. "I

wouldn't have thrown her to the wolves. I love Isolde. Of course I do."

Violet lifted a brow and glanced at Victor, who cleared his throat. "Positives? His supposed fortune?"

"I thought. It might not have been a great match, but it wasn't terrible. Not really. It could have been much worse."

Violet closed her eyes and swallowed back her reaction. Mr. Danvers and his mad-as-a-hatter son had murdered each other over their obsession with Isolde. The younger Mr. Danvers had died in the river.

Violet and her family had thought those times were behind them. Thinking back to that time was enough to make Violet sick. How would Isolde feel? The memory of Isolde shaking in Vi's arms, and whisper-crying over and over again, "Oh god, Vi, thank god. Thank god he's dead. Thank god."

Violet bit down on her bottom lip to shove the memories away, but she couldn't. Jack had been stabbed, they'd been in the Thames in the darkness, they heard the fight in the water and been unable to do anything but hope and pray. She never wanted to think of that time again and it all came back, wrapped up in a bow, while Lady Eleanor—cold fish that she was—was watching.

"I believed Mr. Danvers was acceptable enough," Lady Eleanor said evenly. She cleared her throat. "Perhaps you know that Harry Mathers has escaped jail?"

Violet nodded. Harry Mathers had been Danvers's partner who'd gone to prison for financial crimes. Back when Lady Eleanor pressured Isolde into accepting Danvers's offer, the countess had done so to keep her own secrets safe at the cost of Isolde's potential happiness. "You think he knows what his partner knew about you?"

"I do."

"Why?"

"He's blackmailing me. If your father finds out—" Her gaze was on the floor again. "Well, he can't find out."

"What do they know about you?" Victor demanded.

"I'm not telling you that."

"How did this person deliver his or her demands?"

"In different ways," Lady Eleanor said vaguely. Lady Eleanor was rarely vague.

Violet took in a slow breath and blew it out quietly. Violet stood because she couldn't not stand. She had to move or strangle her stepmother. Vi paced behind the Chesterfield while Victor asked a series of questions that went unanswered as Lady Eleanor wept into her handkerchief.

Vi ignored the tears as she paced. Perhaps Lady Eleanor hadn't wanted her daughter to marry Danvers, but Violet thought it was more likely that Lady Eleanor had known it wouldn't be a happy marriage for Isolde, and Eleanor had talked herself into believing that it would be all right all the same.

"He blackmailed you back then." Violet twisted her wedding ring around her finger as she paced. "He's dead, of course, but either one of his other victims, his partner, or a combination thereof have discovered what he knew."

"Other victims?"

"Of course. He was a rat. If he'd had the chance to twist someone else on his string, he would have. Given that he wasn't a young man—"

"Haven't we covered that?" Lady Eleanor snapped.

"—it wasn't as though he was new to his crimes when he was dealing with you and Isolde. It makes logical sense that you were neither his first victim nor would you have been his last."

"So?" her stepmother wailed. "Why do I care about them?"

No empathy? Violet wanted to demand. No care for mankind in general? No disgust over the very act of crime? Violet fiddled with her ring as she paced, keeping her disgust to herself. "You were hardly unwitting of the name of your blackmailer. You were just arrogant enough to believe that you were the only fish worth catching."

"What did he have on you?" Victor asked Lady Eleanor while she stared at Violet, scowling like a fishwife ready to let loose her rage. "Are there letters or something?"

Lady Eleanor sniffled into her handkerchief. "There were letters between myself and Carlton Danvers about the wedding to Isolde and the reasons behind her engagement."

"You think it's Harry Mathers, but it doesn't have to be." Violet rubbed the back of her neck then reached for her coffee cup for a long drink before speaking. "There might have been others who knew about those things. What about your brothers?"

Lady Eleanor's dark look was the only answer to that question.

"Have you been paying money?"

"Yes," Lady Eleanor said. "I had hoped paying the fiend would silence him."

Victor made a scoffing noise, but when Violet and Lady Eleanor glanced his way, he was sipping innocently from his coffee cup.

"I think it's Mathers," Lady Eleanor said, flushing deeply and avoiding both of their gazes, "as one of the things they want is for Isolde to return to England."

"Why would he care about Isolde? Her over any of the rest of us?" Violet sat and slowly placed her coffee cup on the saucer, set the saucer down with a sharp click, and leaned towards her stepmother, forcing eye contact.

"Harry Mathers hasn't been the same. He wants revenge on Carlton Danvers, but he's dead. His son is dead. All that is left is the woman who had promised to marry Danvers."

"What have you done?" Vi demanded.

"Nothing," Lady Eleanor lied.

CHAPTER 3

"*I*f you told Isolde to come home while Harry Mathers is free, she would be in danger." Victor cursed, rose, and left the room. He had gone from the judgmental, lazy spaniel to the protective older brother.

"Where is he going?" Lady Eleanor wailed. "This isn't what I wanted."

Violet shook her head. Did it need to be explained? Clearly, Victor had determined that an immediate telegram to Tomas and their sister was necessary.

"I know you two! You're like demons," Lady Eleanor shouted, losing all pretense of anything but outrage. "You don't care about anyone but yourself. Isolde will be fine."

"Harry Mathers was declared mad by Mr. Smith. Smith is not a normal man, so if Smith were to declare such a thing, Mathers has descended far beyond whatever line we'd use to judge such a thing. Smith is far more—calloused—about such things."

"I know!" Lady Eleanor shouted. "I know! You told me about Harry Mathers, didn't you? You reminded me of it when you told me and you illustrated it with details. I am not responsible for what Mathers has become."

"No one is saying you're responsible. What we're saying is that bringing Isolde near Mathers is dangerous if he really is obsessing over Danvers and avenues of revenge."

Lady Eleanor stared, jaw clenching. Her hands were fisted and her face was flushed.

"Calling her back here could give him the chance to enact whatever revenge he's been obsessing over," Violet told her clearly, wanting her stepmother to fully understand the situation.

"She has Tomas now. He'll protect her."

"Last time she was in danger, she was taken from a busy street. Tomas can't be with her every second." And there was the child to consider.

Vi took another deep breath in and then let it out. The rage was too much and rather than a slow exhale, Violet sounded like a furious owl. She tried again, but it was useless. Her gaze met Lady Eleanor's.

"Don't look at me like that," her stepmother warned.

Violet bit down on her bottom lip. She wanted to say, I can't help it, but she knew it would come out like an enraged shriek.

"You'll see when you have children," Lady Eleanor told Violet. "Should you ever have children."

Violet ignored the jab.

"You'll see that your love for each child is different. That the drive to protect them hits you differently."

Violet swallowed as she dug her fingernails into her hands.

"Do you think I don't know Geoffrey isn't to everyone's taste?" Lady Eleanor said sharply, grabbing Violet's wrist and digging in her nails. Violet guessed that Lady Eleanor didn't even realize what she was doing. "Do you think I don't see how Isolde is beautiful and everyone loves her? Geoffrey needs me. If Isolde has to sacrifice some of her shine— Well, not all of your children will be brilliant, clever, funny, and likable."

Violet twisted her hand away from her stepmother and hissed, "Do you think I don't know you? Do you think I didn't see how you approached and loved Gerald —Father's heir—while you ignored the rest of us? Even at seven-years-old, I knew why. Gerald would matter to you when the rest of us had left the nest, but Gerald would never leave. The nest would be his. Not yours."

Lady Eleanor gasped and reached back to slap Violet, but Vi caught her stepmother's arm.

"Do you think that we didn't see how you favored Geoffrey even while Isolde was young? No one could know what a wart you'd turn him into. Not then, but still he was your star. Please stop trying to persuade me to see you as a sacrificing mother."

"Fine," Lady Eleanor said, dropping the matter with such quickness that Violet was startled into silence. "Your father can't know about this." She stood and smoothed her dress.

"I am not the repository of your lies. I won't keep your secrets for you. I owe you a favor. Finding out who is blackmailing you is it. Father is your own concern, but I suggest you keep this in mind."

Lady Eleanor glared.

"A SIGNIFICANT AMOUNT of the cleverness of your children and stepchildren comes from him," Violet warned. "He is no cipher and if he turns his attention to your crimes—"

Lady Eleanor paled, hands shaking. Finally, she demanded, "Well?"

Violet had stood to pace again. She had to let loose her energy so she didn't strangle her stepmother. "Well?"

"What are you going to do?"

"What can be done to discover the blackmailer."

"Yes. How are you going to do that?"

Violet blinked as she turned on her stepmother. "I don't know yet. You've hardly done anything more than tell us what you'd tell one of your friends. Vague asides, half-apologies, and ridiculous excuses."

"I want updates. I'll see you every other morning for tea to approve your next course of action. Here is a list of people who don't like me. It's possible that they would have helped Danvers."

Violet took the list, opened it, and then closed it without reading the names or scoffing rudely. "No."

"No?"

"I'm not reporting to you."

"You owe me a favor."

"The favor is helping you at all. I am not yours to command. I will be ruled by caring for the people I love and looking out for them, not by your demands. Victor and I both. Jack as well, should his case ever end."

"You love me?" Lady Eleanor scoffed. "Lies don't become us."

"I don't like you. You don't like me. But I love Isolde and Geoffrey, and they would be hurt by this. Isolde most of all, though I suspect it could be the making or breaking of Geoffrey. I wonder. If he knew that you'd have sacrificed Isolde, would he rise up and become the man he has the potential of becoming or would he cement himself as a wart?"

❧

"I'M A TERRIBLE BROTHER," Victor said as he flopped down onto a chair in the parlor. "I've telephoned Gerald so you can have the one good brother around."

"You are the worst." Violet had continued to pace until Victor arrived. "I suspect either Peter or Lionel were the good brother. I wish they'd survived."

The two of them shared a look. The pain of having lost a pair of siblings before they'd known them resurfaced too often around Lady Eleanor. It wasn't just her fault that Vi and Victor had been sent to Aunt Agatha. Father had let them go because he'd thought it would give them a chance at happiness. They'd thrived with Aunt Agatha and found their happiness again after the loss of their mother.

"I shouldn't have left you alone with her, but my hands were begging to wring her neck." Victor sounded more smug than anything else.

"You should have left," Violet countered. "Who knows if Lady Eleanor would have succeeded in getting Isolde and Tomas to come back to England. However, you should also have come back. After you sent the telegram and made your telephone call. Leaving me with her has earned you several black marks. You, sir, are on a very rocky road."

"I'm a terrible brother," he repeated lazily and without remorse. "Want to go dancing tonight? Algie has sent by a note. It was on the table there in the hall. Must've come after Lady Eleanor. He says he saw we'd come home and wants to have a bit of a gossip. I invited Gerald to join us. He also wants to speak with us. Everyone we know wants to have a gossip."

"I thought Algie was in America. And how would he know we'd returned when we haven't been out?"

"I'm guessing that either he's back or he didn't go. Apparently he witnessed Hargreaves's arrival. He says he's taken to stopping by our houses and make sure they look all right when we aren't around."

"What a pet!" Violet laughed. "Doesn't he realize we've hired a few blokes to do just that?"

"Clearly not," Victor grinned.

Violet reopened the list of 'people who don't like me' from Lady Eleanor and with a twist to her lips, added Violet Wakefield, Jack Wakefield, and Victor Carlyle to the list. Vi folded the list up and tossed it to her brother.

He opened it, read the list and then lifted a brow.

"We do need Gerald," Victor told Violet. "He might be lazy."

"He is."

"He might be spoilt."

"He is."

"He might be our brother."

"He is."

"If I say that he might be—"

"He is," Violet said, grinning as Victor groaned.

"Your jokes are terrible, but he does live in the same house as Lady Eleanor. If anyone has an idea of what she's been up to, or how the notes are coming in—"

Violet gasped. "I once more prove that I'm a valuable beyond rubies."

"Not that again," Victor snapped even though she could tell he was half-amused. "How long until Tomas replies? I'm worried. What if they were already coming? You know what we need?"

"The ability to tell Isolde everything without feeling like we're destroying her personally? The answer to the question for what this will do to Geoffrey?" Violet frowned deeply and then said, "Father wouldn't have let Isolde marry Danvers if he'd known that his wife was blackmailed into pushing for the wedding. But does he know now? If he does, do you think he really loves her? Would whatever she's hiding destroy him?"

"Yes, we need all that," Victor agreed, "and John Smith."

"I think we might need more than Smith," Violet countered.

"Do we?"

"He is clever when it comes to finding out secrets, but we need to know how Harry Mathers got out of jail. We need to know who could possibly be aware of Lady Eleanor's secrets. We need to know what her secrets are, so we can handle the fact that they'll eventually come out."

"I don't know," Victor mused, taking the last of the coffee. "I'm not sure I can handle her secrets."

Violet ignored him. "We need to also know who both knows her well and is also unscrupulous enough to blackmail her."

"Surely everyone Lady Eleanor actually likes," Victor suggested helpfully and then ignored Violet's exasperated look.

"She gave us nothing but orders and, well—we can't even call them half-truths. She gave us shreds of nothing mixed with scraps of truth. "

Victor shifted and then rubbed his hands over his face and his expression changed. The teasing dropped and seriousness returned. "She did give us nothing. We need the details about how she was blackmailed. She's decided it is Harry Mathers blackmailing her—"

"He must be involved," Violet groaned. "It's not like you can walk out of prison. There must have been outside help, and who would help him willingly?"

"If it isn't Mathers who is engineering things—"

"He could be a patsy." Violet grinned at her brother. "He could have been freed in order to provide cover for someone else."

"Or," Victor said, "he could have been freed because he's providing us such an excellent distraction."

Violet rolled her eyes at her brother with a solid smack on his shoulder for repeating what she said. He grinned, so delighted at his teasing that Violet knew instantly he was going to carry on with it.

"What about Jack and Ham? Can we call them home?"

Violet shook her head. "Victor, whatever we're working on is nothing compared to what they're working on. We can't distract them."

"What is happening up there?"

"Jack isn't going to tell me if it's bad. I can hardly sleep with the cases we've come across as it is and I haven't even seen half the bodies we've been involved with. Jack has been carefully silent."

Victor winced as Violet went back to pacing. She didn't want to think about Jack's case. If she let her mind linger too long on it, her imagination would start filling in holes with the grisly and horrific.

"Having an imagination is a curse," Violet told Victor. "I don't understand why you don't also suffer."

Victor said, "I do now."

"Now?"

"Being a father is—" Victor shook his head. "Terrifying."

"So you didn't love me enough to suffer before now."

"I was just assured of our mutual immortality. Do you know how many ways a baby can die? Bad sniffles, dead. The influenza, dead. A bad fall, dead. They're so delicate. They can crawl into a fire. They could so easily be taken away from me."

"They won't be."

"We both know that you can't promise that, Vi."

Their gazes met and no more words were necessary.

CHAPTER 4

"So, Algie?" Violet changed the subject for both of their peace of mind.

"Algie," Victor nodded, voice tremulous.

"Dinner?" Vi asked. "Tonight? Do we have reservations?"

"He said he'd take care of it," Victor answered vaguely. At her dark look he added, "Reservations at 9:00 p.m., drinks and dancing after. You'll have to dance with me, old girl. He's bringing that rich wife of his."

Violet smacked her brother again. "Pretty demon, pretty devil, darling Vi are all acceptable. Old girl? No."

"All right, all right, old girl," he said, dodging her next smack. "I worked from 2:00 to 4:00 a.m. and wrote a large number of likely unintelligible pages since I am a delicate flower who requires my wife to sleep. It'll take me a bit to adjust and be able to churn out something readable."

"Agreed," Violet said. "I also wrote during that time.

Shall we shuffle our pages and just see if we can pull out something worthwhile?"

"As good a plan as anything else."

She grinned at him, rang the bell, and called for fresh coffee and fresh sandwiches, along with an excess of chocolates. She felt as though she needed a chocolate treat with her favorite drink to recover from the visit with her stepmother. Together the twins worked on their story rather than pursue inquiries into the blackmailing, mostly out of spite and the necessity of a break after dealing with Lady Eleanor. Something of a palate cleanser.

"Well," Victor asked, "should we stop with the continuing story of young Isla, our married ingénue?'

Violet grinned. "Funny how we've returned to a story that was based off of Isolde now that we're dealing with the same issues once again. I have to admit, I look forward to her reaction."

"Hilarious," Victor said sourly. He left the room and returned with Hargreaves and a chalkboard.

"Must we?" Vi demanded.

"Don't," he said as Violet stood to help, "it's my turn." She frowned, and he eyed her harshly. "Violet, it's hard for me to say this, but you're greedy with the chalk and the chalkboard. An intellectual glutton, if you will."

She stared at him for a long moment and then crossed her legs and leaned back, waving at him to proceed.

"By all means," she said dryly, "accept my deepest apologies."

"Indeed," he told her, "as if you were the only one capable of operating a chalkboard."

They looked at each other with the corner of his mouth twitching as he fought back his reaction.

"You forgot how to be a brother without a baby in your arms or a wife saying, Victor. Who will idly scold you now that you're free?"

"How dare you, madam?" he scolded. "Feels like I'm putting on an old suit, to be honest. One that doesn't quite fit the same anymore."

Violet shook her head at him and then took out Lady Eleanor's list of names to read it over again. "You know we can't trust this."

"Oh, I know," Victor agreed. He lifted his brow and eyed her quizzically. "Our names weren't on it. It wasn't complete until you added them. Honestly, I can think of a good half-dozen folks who should be at the top of this list that aren't on it at all."

"She's so difficult." Violet sighed, stretching her neck as Victor copied the list onto the chalkboard.

Harry Mathers

Genevieve Bromley

Lisa Van Lyden

Charlotte Wilder

George Terrance

"This tells us nothing," Victor said after transcribing the list to the chalkboard. "In fact, the only thing I realize as I write this is that I don't believe it. Who are these people?"

"Well," Violet told him as she considered, "Harry Mathers is the partner of Isolde's once-intended who was murdered on their wedding day."

"Be quiet," Victor replied idly.

"Mathers's daughter was in a relationship with his

partner, though poor Mathers was unaware. His grand-child has been put up for adoption. He got arrested, despite the care he used in keeping himself separate from Danvers's crimes, because Jack and Ham kept looking for evidence, found it, and then testified against him."

"Yes, thank you," Victor said dryly. "Thank you for telling me all of the things I already knew. Isn't Genevieve Bromley the daughter of that rich man? What's his name?"

"Noah Bromley. He's quite powerful, I believe. And certainly rich. Epically so. Why would his daughter be Lady Eleanor's enemy?"

"I don't know," Victor said, rolling his eyes at her. "Who is this Lisa woman? Or this Charlotte Wilder? They could be friends or girls or children of friends or random names she created to disguise whatever she was doing that she's being blackmailed over."

"What about George Terrace? Does that seem familiar?"

"I think he's a crony of Father's. Though—I really don't know. For all I know, he's the fellow who delivers the fish."

"Very helpful," Violet said. "Perhaps Gerald will know."

In her opinion, writing was a way to discover her thoughts. It was why her journal and the chalkboards worked so well for her. They helped her digest what she already knew in a way that allowed her to consider it from different angles. Even in recapping what was happening in her life, she found new ideas and caught holes in her thought process, but Victor wasn't trying to discover anything. He was trying to lighten Violet's mood.

Violet rose and left him to his teasing, crossing to the stacks of pages of their manuscript. She skimmed her own again to see what she'd done the night before and then read his with careful attention. As she worked through the two sets of circumstances, it occurred to her that they should have been a little more focused on laying out a plan to write this book.

They were out of practice in writing in the same manner when they were in each other's pockets. They needed to re-organize their process. She glanced over and saw him pacing in front of the chalkboard and snorted softly. He'd been caught by his own teasing.

"I can't make heads or tails of it."

"We aren't going to on our own, I don't think," Vi told him as she crossed to stand next to him. "She's clearly lying. We need to find out the real truth, but I don't know how we do that. Even if we pin her down with one truth, she'll lie about another."

"The most important thing to Lady Eleanor is her image and her status," Victor said. "Possibly young Geoffrey takes a slight precedence, but Isolde doesn't. The rest of us don't. Father certainly doesn't."

Gerald arrived just as Violet poured herself another cup of Turkish coffee. Gerald was older than Violet and Victor by about a decade, putting him well into his 30s. The twins got their coloring, the sharpness of their features, and their slenderness from their mother. Unlike them, Gerald was bluff, blonde, ruddy-cheeked, and given to just a little extra weight. He was a large and strong man, but he was covered in a layer of fat.

He glanced between them as he entered. "I feel as though I've flashed back in time. What are you doing here? Where is Jack? Is Kate still helping her mother?"

"Yes," Victor answered and Violet said, "Jack is in Leeds working on something dark and terrible if the tone of his letters is of any indication."

"So you two decided to flashback in time." Gerald crossed and dropped a kiss on Violet's head and then shook Victor's hand. Gerald grinned at Victor with delight and then his gaze landed on the chalkboard. The frown started before he'd even started reading, but it deepened as he read over the list of names. "What's all this? Why are you two meddling with Lottie? How do you even know her?"

"Who's Lottie? Charlotte Wilder?"

Gerald's mouth was down-turned, showing lines that Violet had never noticed before on her brother's face. "She's the woman I've asked to be my wife." He scowled deeply, eyes agonized. "She hasn't answered me. She won't talk to me at all."

Violet cursed as Victor groaned. The twins met each other's eyes and they both jumped to the terrible conclusion that Lady Eleanor was meddling again. What if she'd stepped beyond meddling with a step—like she had with Violet—to the future stepchild's spouse? Lady Eleanor had tried with Jack, but with Gerald, the heir, what wouldn't Lady Eleanor do?

"Why is my Lottie on a list with Harry Mathers? I assure you that Lottie does not know Mathers."

"She's not," Violet told him. "She's on a list of Lady Eleanor's enemies."

Gerald paled. "Bloody hell." The following cursing

streak was enough to give the twins the impression of where Lady Eleanor stood on the matter.

"Are you all right, old man?" Victor asked Gerald, taking him by the arm and shoving him into a chair. "I'll get you a coffee."

Gerald swallowed dryly. "I'll need something stronger than that."

Victor crossed to the bar in the parlor and poured Gerald a stiff whiskey. Their oldest brother took the glass with shaking hands. "Lottie won't talk to me. I thought—I thought—I'd done something to anger her. You don't think—"

The twins looked at each other, but said nothing. They did, in fact, think that their stepmother had intervened.

Gerald took a large drink of the whiskey. Their brother's voice was frantic and speedy when he spoke. "I've sent flowers. I've sent chocolates. Jewelry. Vague apologies. Pleas for her to tell me what is wrong, but she won't speak to me at all."

Violet's gaze narrowed and she rose sharply. "What is her telephone number?"

Gerald's hand was still shaking as he answered. "What are you going to do?"

Violet patted his shoulder. "Sometimes a woman will talk to another woman. I'll see if I can help."

He was silent, but his gaze was desperate. He gave over the telephone number with a trembling voice.

Violet patted him on the shoulder once again before she left the parlor and had the operator connect her. "Charlotte Wilder, please."

"This is she."

"This is Violet Wakefield. Do you know who I am?"

There was a very long silence and then finally a hushed, "Yes."

"I understand there is something wrong between you and Gerald." Violet paused when Charlotte Wilder did not reply. "Whatever is wrong between you and my brother is most likely based off of lies and manipulations of Lady Eleanor Carlyle."

Charlotte did not answer, but she did not disconnect either.

"I'd like to help you resolve the problem between you and my brother. If you love Gerald, perhaps it will comfort you to know that I can assure you that he loves you and he is miserable without you. I can also assure you that whatever obstacle Lady Eleanor put between yourself and him can be overcome."

"I'm not sure I believe that," the quiet voice replied, confirming Lady Eleanor's involvement. "There is more than you know."

"Will you give me a chance?"

"What do you want from me?"

"I'll send an auto for you. Come and talk to me."

"I—"

"I'm going to call you Lottie because I choose to believe we'll be sisters. As your sister, Lottie, I'll help you find your heart and give it back to my brother. I assure you he deserves it."

"I—"

"Please," Violet begged.

"It's not just me," Lottie whispered. "I wish it were only me, but it's not—and, and I can't."

"Charlotte Wilder," Violet snapped, "you can't let the monster win!"

"That's your stepmother." Lottie sounded shocked.

"Who would know better than I what we're dealing with? The auto will be there within the hour. At least give me a chance."

Violet hung up before Lottie could say no and sent the auto with Hargreaves and his perfect ability to be gentle, proper, and insistent.

CHAPTER 5

*V*iolet had no idea what to expect when she imagined the woman Gerald might love, but it wasn't Charlotte Wilder. The girl—woman—who approached the door was quite young, though not so young that there was anything untoward. Her eyes were blue, her hair was dark. She ignored fashion and the typical bob for long silky curls, and Violet had little doubt it was because her hair was a shining crown on her head. Her skin was very pale but also very freckled.

Lottie's dress was blue and not particularly expensive. Her lips were pink. Her cheeks were too pale for a general aura of healthiness, and she trembled when Violet took her hand. That being said, Charlotte Wilder —even as sad as she seemed—was lively. Violet had the image of a woman whose natural state was one of sheer cheerfulness.

Violet did not take Lottie into the parlor with her brothers but quietly led the way into the library where a fire had been lit. The puppies had been brought into the room, and Violet locked the door behind them. Vi wasn't going to have Gerald throwing himself at Lottie's feet until Violet knew why Lottie was running from a man like Gerald Carlyle. He was, to put it very bluntly, a catch.

Lottie took the seat Violet nodded towards, and then Violet reached down and put a puppy in her lap.

"Oh." Lottie looked down and ran her fingers over the puppy's belly and repeated, "Ohhh."

"Indeed," Violet agreed as she sat, lifting Rouge into her lap instead of one of the puppies. Rouge put her paws on Violet's shoulders and licked her chin once before rubbing her face into Vi's neck and giving her a woebegone moan. Vi laughed as she told Lottie, "Rouge objects to not being at my feet all day. She's a good mama, but she wants me to know that she misses me. She'd prefer I climb into the basket with them and we all snuggle in a pile together until they're big enough to send on their way."

"That sounds lovely." Lottie's voice was shaking. She had a tremulous hope in her gaze, but the overall feel of her expression was one of despair.

"Do you love my brother?" Violet didn't belabor the point of their conversation.

Lottie nodded silently. A single tear rolled down her face. The single tear on Lottie's face was heart-breaking while the single tear earlier from Lady Eleanor was incapable of drawing an ounce of emotion.

"Tell me about it." Vi's gentle voice had Lottie meeting her gaze, searching it desperately.

"He never should have taken up with me."

Violet ignored the statement. "How did you meet?" Violet trailed her fingers over Rouge's ears.

"I met him at the park. I was walking our neighbor's dog. He slipped his leash to chase a squirrel. I was chasing the dog. Gerald caught him."

"It sounds kismet," Violet said with a smile, watching Lottie carefully as another tear rolled down her cheek.

Lottie's voice was trembling when she shook her head and answered, "I'm just a bank manager's daughter, and the earl keeps his funds in the bank where Daddy works. If I—if I—"

"If you marry Gerald, then your father will be put out of a job?" Lady Eleanor wasn't even clever. It was a blunt instrument for destroying the relationship. Any woman Gerald would love would sacrifice herself for her family.

"Please don't play games with me," Lottie snapped with a surprising amount of anger. "There is an understanding between him and Genevieve Bromley. Miss Bromley doesn't care if I'm his…his…mistress, but I care. I don't even know why I'm here. He's going to marry that Bromley girl and I won't be his—his whore."

Violet laughed, hardly surprised by the depth of her stepmother's despicable lies. It was a mean sound, and it startled Lottie.

"You're just like her," Lottie said, standing. She couldn't escape quickly with the puppy in her hands. She turned to put the little thing in the basket, giving Vi time to catch her.

"I assure you," Violet told Lottie, taking her wrist before she could put the puppy down, "I am not. I also assure you that Gerald Carlyle may be lazy, but he is also my brother. He's upstanding and kind. He would never in his life take a mistress."

Lottie was quiet for a moment, taking that in. "It doesn't change the fact of Daddy's position."

"Gerald would hardly let that get in the way of love."

"Your father cares."

"My father doesn't care that my husband is a detective."

"You aren't the heir."

"And I'm possibly the least favored child, so you have a point there," Violet told Lottie evenly. Lottie's gaze widened. "My father prefers his sons over his daughters. It's always been clear. He'd come visit my twin and me, take me for an ice cream, drop me back at school, and spend the rest of the visit with Victor. But understand, Victor is the least favorite son. The two of us have made peace with our standing a long time ago. It's like a scarred-over wound on our hearts."

Lottie blinked rapidly, trying to follow Violet's statement. It wasn't that it was hard to understand--it was just so rife with emotion.

"The thing is," Violet continued, "as you age, you realize that what seems like a cruel blow of being the unwanted child is quite a blessing later. My sister Isolde, the favored daughter, almost married a criminal because of the interference of my stepmother."

Lottie gasped.

"Father probably would have fought Gerald's attraction to you years ago," Vi continued, "but Gerald is in his mid-thirties. He has shown no interest in the women they've been throwing before him for all his adult life. I have little doubt that Father tried ordering him to marry.

Gerald is, after all the heir, and Father wouldn't want the least favorite son to inherit."

"Yes. To Miss Bromley. I told you."

"Gerald would have told him, 'No.'"

"You can't know that."

"Of course I can. I know him rather well for all our distance. He's not a hard book to crack. He's lazy, spoilt, and stubborn. He told Victor once that he'd die alone before he'd marry another 'Lady Eleanor' and recommended my brother marry before Father realized Gerald's intention to remain a bachelor."

"He didn't." Lottie looked shocked.

"I assure you, he did. If Miss Bromley is recommended by Lady Eleanor, Gerald would never, ever consider the woman. Never."

"I—" There was dawning hope in her eyes. "You think you know him that well?"

"Lady Eleanor sees all of her stepchildren and her daughter as commodities to raise her status or the status of her precious son, Geoffrey. That includes Gerald."

"But—"

"You have to understand," Violet told Lottie gently, tugging her back to the chair, pressing her handkerchief in her hands, and placing two puppies on her lap this time. Violet struggled to find a way to describe it. Finally, she asked, "Do you have a good mother?"

Lottie nodded in jerky, surprised movements.

"Lady Eleanor is not a good mother. If you judge her by your own mother's standards, you are giving Lady Eleanor a credit that is simply ridiculous. She loves her own children to the best of her ability, but that doesn't say much."

Violet sat down, scooting towards Lottie and taking both of her hands. In a low, intimate voice, Violet said, "Eleanor Carlyle manipulated her daughter into marrying a man twice her age, fat, and entirely unappealing in order to keep unsavory details about herself out of the public purview."

Lottie's gaze narrowed.

"She's the type of woman who will endlessly attempt to keep Gerald from marrying, despite the fact that my twin would be the heir. She wants the illusion that it could be Geoffrey to make the best match for him. As long as Victor only has daughters, she can build up the illusion. To do so, she will lie, perhaps claiming that Kate can't have more children or awful rumors about Gerald. Who knows how she intends to go about it, but I assure you—she has a plan."

Lottie bit down on her bottom lip. "I still can't put my daddy at risk. I'm the oldest. There are six more children in my family who need him to have a good position. I'll—I'll find someone else."

"Or, you could marry the man you love, who loves you."

"My daddy—"

"Your daddy will continue to have work."

"He won't take a handout, Mrs. Wakefield. If you are wrong, my daddy won't work for you, and my siblings could go hungry."

"First of all," Violet told Lottie, "that's ridiculous. A good father and husband would take a position if it meant securing his family, regardless of his pride. Second of all, Lady Eleanor does not speak for Father. She does, however, pretend to do so. My father would never have an honorable man removed from his position."

"But—"

"But, Lady Eleanor lies," Violet said very precisely. "Frequently."

Lottie paused and then carefully picked up each puppy and set them on the ground. Vi scooped them up and put them in the basket.

"I can tell when Gerald lies," Lottie told Violet.

"A very useful skill when you love someone lazy and spoiled. It also tells me that you have not spoken to him about Miss Bromley."

Lottie looked away, biting her lip.

"You should test him," Violet said. "Face to face. Have him declare himself. If he does so in front of me and Victor, you can trust it. And you'll see that he isn't lying about his feelings for you. Gerald is a very good older brother." She paused. "He's here, you know."

Lottie started and then paused, rubbing her hand along the back of her neck, obviously at war with herself. Her love for Gerald won over her fears. "May I speak with him? Will you bring him here?"

Violet led Lottie to the parlor. They were sitting side-by-side, smoking, feet up, the scent of whiskey combining with tobacco. Neither of her brothers had realized Lottie had arrived.

"Oh!" Violet groaned. "Behold the wallowing of mankind."

Victor waved the smoke out of his face and his eyes widened as he took in Lottie Wilder half-hidden behind Violet. Gerald, however, didn't even open his eyes, and sank back on the sofa in a self-pitying stupor.

"Don't harass me, Vi," Gerald groaned. "You don't understand."

"I understand far more than you realize," Vi replied, hooking her arm through Lottie's and dragging her into the room. "The road between Jack and myself wasn't easy."

"Gah," Gerald sighed with resignation, still with his eyes closed.

"You know Lady Eleanor doesn't like Jack even now. Even though she'd prefer for him to be here helping her with her little issue. She'd just also prefer that events end with me leaving him to marry some downtrodden, money-grubbing, third son of a duke."

"You'll never do that," Gerald said miserably, squeezing his eyelids tight in pain. "She gave up on you long ago. She'll never let me be. Not me. Not the heir."

Violet turned to Lottie, who was standing silently, hands clutched so tightly that she had left white rings under her fingertips. It was only her grip that was keeping her hands from overtly shaking.

"Ahh—" Victor said. "Gerald, old man—"

"I'm wallowing!" Gerald whined. "Lottie won't speak to me. For some reason you two are meddling for Lady Eleanor, that shrew! Father has taken off for the hills, once again leaving his be-damned wife behind. I need a wallow." The last was a bit of a groan. "I will wallow in my misery, drink heavily of Jack's excellent whiskey—"

"That's mine," Violet lied, but Gerald scoffed and sloshed whiskey from his cup into his mouth, putting the back of his hand across his eyes, heedless of the burning cigarette. "Go away, Violet."

"You could sit up, put out your cigarette, and explain

to Lottie that you want her and only her. That you don't want to marry that Bromley daughter and set up Lottie as your piece on the side."

Gerald sat up to stare at Violet, aghast. "Why would she think that?" His tone was a mixture of horror and outrage. It was only then that he saw Lottie.

"Please, Gerald?" Lottie asked with desperate hope.

Gerald leapt so quickly from his seat that he sprayed Victor with the remnants of his glass of whiskey.

Violet calmly leaned down and lifted the burning cigarette from her carpet. "Come, Victor, these two must speak, and we really should change for dinner." Vi looked back to where Gerald was standing, mouth agape, staring in shock and hope at Lottie. "I suspect Gerald will stand us up, the fiend."

Their older brother glanced at Violet, his gaze shining brightly with gratitude.

"Talk to her," Violet told him quietly. "You threw her in with the sharks without enough preparation, Gerald, this is your chance to make this right." She led Victor out of the parlor.

"Is that Lottie?" Victor whispered too loud. "It must be. I didn't think you'd get her here. Gerald said he's been begging."

"Women have ways, darling Victor." She paused for a long moment and then rubbed her hands down the back of her neck. Her shoulders were tense and pained just watching the couple. "I know I added myself to the list for Lady Eleanor, but we need to add Gerald."

Victor shook his head. "Gerald would never help Harry Mathers get out of prison."

"Neither would either of us. What if those things

49

aren't connected? We're blindfolded in the dark, Victor. We don't even know that Lady Eleanor really has been blackmailed. She never told us what she was being black-mailed over, where she received her blackmail threats or the nature of what she's been paying. Has she been leaving jewels, draining her pin money, stealing from Father? We have no idea."

CHAPTER 6

*V*iolet dressed carefully, hoping that her dress would make her feel bright and happy. She wasn't blue in her spirits, for which she was intensely grateful. She'd focused her will on getting good sleep, moving her body regularly, and concentrating on gratitude and positivity. She wrote in her journal regularly and used the confidantes that were available to her to work out her worries. She couldn't make the blues never arrive again, but she'd been successful in finding ways to fight those feelings.

Alone, however, her mind turned to Jack. Was he all right? She knew the case was bothering him, but was he in danger? She reminded herself that Jack had survived the Great War. He was a Scotland Yard detective with his best friend backing him and they were both among the best detectives that England had to offer.

Violet fiddled with her wedding ring before finishing her dressing. She pulled on black stockings and then glanced through her evening gowns until she found a grey dress embroidered with diamonds and beaded with black swirls. Grey and black? The colors didn't feel depressing but elegant. Violet wound her black pearls around her neck, adding a pearl and diamond choker, a pearl and black ribbon headpiece, and diamond earbobs. She put bangles on both wrists and then added her spider ring to her forefinger. It was past Halloween, but Vi loved the ring and it amused her greatly. Violet applied shadow around her eyes, drew on her eyebrows, blackened her lashes, and blended rouge into her cheeks and lips.

Violet put on her pair of black shoes and smiled at herself in the mirror. She had missed these times with Victor. It was no time to focus on worrying about Jack. She had to trust him to his skills and God and allow herself to have fun with Victor and Algie.

Violet took a clutch and joined Victor downstairs. He was standing just outside the parlor door shamelessly listening to Gerald. Hargreaves held Violet's coat and she slipped it on and then crossed to Victor to push the point of her shoe into the back of his knee.

He stumbled and then turned and grinned at her. In a low voice he asked, "Do you remember when I begged Kate to marry me?"

Vi nodded. Of course she did. It was one of her favorite memories.

"Gerald is far, far better at begging," Victor said.

"Is Lottie crueler? Kate said yes to you quickly."

"Lottie was vicious," Victor whispered loudly. "She made him swear to her that he didn't love or want the Bromley girl and she also made him beg. On his knees."

"You were wise enough to not introduce Kate to Lady Eleanor until after you had Kate's commitment," Vi whispered back as loudly. "Our intrepid future earl was not so wise."

"Go away," Gerald called. "You two are ridiculous."

"This is my house." Violet stuck her head around the door, winking at Lottie. Vi studied the two sitting together on the Chesterfield long enough to note Gerald's arm around Lottie's shoulders, their fingers tangled, and evidence of tears. And just as evidently, the matter between them had been settled in Gerald's favor.

"Did she do this to you?" Lottie asked Victor. They all knew she meant Lady Eleanor by the way Lottie said 'she,' as though afraid saying her name would conjure the beast. There was enough of a tremor in Lottie's voice that Violet had to fight the rush of rage.

Victor's head tilted as he smiled gently at Lottie. "I'm the least important sibling."

"Not to me," Violet told him, hooking her arm through Victor's. "Even if you're stealing my title. Who cares about the future earl?"

"I do," Lottie said shyly.

"Oh!" Violet said, grinning at her brother. "Look at that! Someone is on your side."

"Are you going to be irritating endlessly?" he asked her.

"Lottie and I are valuable beyond rubies," Violet replied and in unison both Gerald and Victor groaned.

"Having returned your love to you is quite the act of service," Violet reminded him. "Rubies would be an excellent choice."

"This is what comes from having spoiled her," Gerald

told Victor. "Vi should be grateful for my sheer notice. As the future earl, my gratitude is incredibly valuable. Why are you doing this?" He gestured to the chalkboard. "What did you say? Stepmother's enemies?"

They all looked at the list of names on the chalkboard.

"What's happening with Lady Eleanor?" Violet countered. "What do you know?"

"What are you doing for her, Vi?" The hatred in Gerald's voice had Vi wincing for her stepmother. But only a little.

Violet nibbled her bottom lip as she considered how to reply, already wishing she hadn't promised to keep Lady Eleanor's secrets.

"Vi owes her a favor," Victor answered. His tone was equally disgusted, but there was no doubt that Victor was on Violet's side. He always was.

"Why?" Gerald demanded.

"She threw that party for Vi that helped catch that prankster."

"And that's causing this?" Gerald asked, gesturing again at the chalkboards. "This is what you do when you're meddling in Jack's cases."

Lottie's gaze was wide with shock, looking between the siblings, but she didn't say a word.

"Don't worry, Lottie," Violet told her. "You'll understand all the details. We have to go."

"What is the limit of this favor?" Gerald wouldn't let the matter drop.

"I wasn't bright enough to set a limit," Violet admitted. "Has she been acting odd lately?"

"I avoid her," Gerald replied. "She takes breakfast in

her room. I don't linger at the house and spend rather a lot of time at my club."

"Why don't you move?" Victor asked.

"Father didn't want me to." Gerald rubbed his thumb over the back of Lottie's wrist. "I'll be sending my man to find me something soon. Lottie won't be living with Lady Eleanor once we marry."

The grandfather clock rang and Violet met Victor's gaze. It was past time to go. Violet leaned down and hugged Lottie and told Gerald, "Make good choices."

His scowl made Lottie laugh and Victor also leaned down and hugged Lottie. "Welcome to the family, Lottie. We're all a little mad here."

~

ALGIE STOOD as Violet and Victor approached the table. His grin was wide and happy and he hugged them both tightly. "I have missed you!"

"We haven't been gone that long, Algie."

"Yes, yes, but I needed help, and you were gone. Had to ask the wife, don't you know? Makes a man feel a bit like a blighter when he has to turn to the old ball and chain for help."

Victor laughed as he seated Vi and greeted Algie's wife, Clara. She was a tiny blonde that made one think of pixies. Quite pretty and delicate, and Algie looked at her with eyes that shone with adoration.

Victor snorted before he admitted, "I ask Kate and Vi for help regularly."

Algie grinned happily. "It's why I turned to my beloved. Thought to myself, what would Victor do and knew he'd dump the problem on the ladies in his life, so I did the same."

His wife laughed and the look she gave him was overly fond despite his high-pitched giggle. Vi quite wanted to put her hand over Algie's mouth and demand a low chuckle or perhaps some sort of mocking huff, but not that girlish giggle.

"What happened?" Vi asked as she accepted the wine that was poured for her. "Why did you need Victor and me?"

"Being blackmailed, aren't I?" Algie giggled once again and his wife looked at him rather fondly for such a statement. "So ridiculous."

"I'm sorry. What did you say?" Violet repeated, glancing at her twin and then back to her cousin.

"You know I'm a bit of a dim idiot. Never more so before I married Clara. Opportunities to blackmail Algie Allyn abound, I fear."

Clara laughed. "Only if you care, darling."

"Yes, well—that's what we did."

"I don't understand," Victor said. "What did you do?"

"The only person whose reaction could really bother our life is Daddy," Clara told him. "So we just told him. Daddy was so upset about some blighter trying to poke a spoke in our wheels that he bypassed the knowledge of Algie's misdeeds and went straight for revenge. We tried finding the fellow, but I fear we failed."

"Old man's planning to come and take care of it himself," Algie sighed. "Clara and I are considering fleeing, but the man is supernatural. Told us if we did, he'd keep the next quarter's allowance. I fear we'll have to ride it out. We tend to run a little tight towards the end. I fear we need that allowance to continue our lifestyle, pay our bills, all those things. You'd think I'd have learned to set a bit by for a rainy day by now, but I haven't."

"What happened?" Victor asked, glancing between the couple in wonder. "You didn't pay the blackmailer, so—"

"Nothing yet," Algie said, giggling again. He did, now that Vi thought about it, sound a bit hysterical.

"When is it supposed to happen?" Victor demanded, but Violet didn't care so much about that answer.

Her own thoughts had moved past Algie to Lady Eleanor. Surely whoever was blackmailing Algernon Allyn was also the same person blackmailing Lady Eleanor. What were the chances that there were two blackmailers working amongst London's upper-crust?

There was not much of an overlap between Algernon Allyn and Lady Eleanor. The twin's cousin was related to them through their mother who had long since died. Lady Eleanor had always seemed retroactively jealous of the late Penelope Allyn, so any links between the two families had faded quickly.

How was it then that Algie and Lady Eleanor were both being blackmailed? Surely it was by the same person? Violet twisted her wedding ring on her finger as her mind traveled along all the linking paths between Algie and Lady Eleanor.

"Vi?"

She nibbled on her bottom lip, not really hearing Victor.

"Vi."

Vi blinked rapidly and glanced up at the others who were all looking at her.

"Someone else we know is being blackmailed. They're

being scrooge-ish with the details. What can you tell us about how you got your blackmail demand?"

"I dunno really. Just appeared in my pocket at the theater. Always so crowded there. Could have been anyone."

"The theater?" Victor asked. "Box seats?"

Algie nodded.

Violet glanced at her twin. He was thinking the same thing. Lady Eleanor adored going to the theater. She hated the plays themselves, but she did like seeing her friends and putting herself on display. She had a regular box. It was possible that she was also being caught there.

"Maybe we can go with you next time," Violet suggested to Algie, who nodded with a grin.

"We've got seats for tomorrow night," he said. "They're doing Twelfth Night. Why is it that Shakespeare had so many plays about fellows dressed up as ladies and the reverse? Ridiculous."

Violet sipped her wine. She didn't want to turn her thoughts to the bard. She played with her wedding ring as she considered what she knew. She slowly realized that she wasn't that close with either Algie or Lady Eleanor. If there was an overlap in their friends, acquaintances, or even servants, Violet wouldn't be able to tell.

Violet shook off her thoughts and asked, "Do you know Charlotte Wilder?"

Algie glanced at Clara to check with her. Slowly they both shook their heads.

Because Victor understood what Violet was doing, he asked, "What about Genevieve Bromley?"

Again they looked at each other before they answered. Another negative.

"George Terrance? Lisa Van Lyden?"

This time the couple both shook their heads without needing to confirm.

"Are they being blackmailed too?" Clara asked.

"Not really," Violet said obliquely. She needed to safeguard all connection to Lady Eleanor or they'd never hear the end of it. "What are we eating?"

CHAPTER 7

*V*iolet wrote Jack a letter the next morning
catching him up on the events since they'd
arrived back in London. She asked him vaguely about
his case with clearer demands that he be careful. She
knew that he'd note the vague inquiries and answer with
equal vagueness which was what she needed and
intended.

She hurried to the ballroom where they had gym
equipment and worked with her jiu-jitsu instructor.
Often Kate, when she was home, joined her. That
morning Beatrice did.

"Beatrice, love," Violet said, "have you seen Mr. Smith
lately?"

"Why would I see him?"

"He seemed intrigued by you."

Beatrice avoided Violet's gaze as she stretched. Violet
waiting, knowing the silence would put pressure on
Beatrice and that the woman would be inclined to

answer anything Violet asked. It wasn't fair to her, Violet knew, but she needed to hunt up the man rather quickly.

"He's been known to catch the same bus as I take," Beatrice muttered to her knees. "If I happen to be going to Mr. Frederick's office or for a meeting. Especially in the evening."

"Not always?"

Beatrice shook her head.

"Would it be too much to ask you to call him and ask him to visit Victor and me?"

Beatrice paused for a moment and then nodded her head. "I can take care of that for you, Mrs.—" Beatrice cleared her throat and then said, "Violet."

"You need to get used to saying my name, Beatrice. You're a professional woman now. The men you're dealing with need to know it."

Beatrice nodded and they both rose when the jiu-jitsu instructor arrived.

John Smith appeared at Violet's door later that afternoon. He followed Hargreaves into the library where Violet and Victor were considering how to pin down Lady Eleanor. He glanced around and then asked, "No Beatrice?"

"She has other duties," Violet told him. He was as pretty as an angel and had the mind of a devil. Violet both liked him and felt certain that he was not good enough for Beatrice.

"Are you going to warn me off of her?"

"I was warned away from Jack. Did you know? It turns out that I knew what was best for me. I won't warn you off of her, but I will caution you that if she doesn't want you and you ignore her wants, I'll crush you."

"And if she doesn't tell me to go away?"

"Mr. Smith, I like you, against my better judgement. Perhaps she does as well. I am neither her mother nor her keeper. I am, however, her friend."

Mr. Smith glanced between the twins and then asked Victor, "What about you?"

"Violet's friends are my friends."

"What do you need?" Smith asked, changing the subject. If he'd been seeking an answer, perhaps he'd gotten it. Or perhaps, he'd break into their house and search through their things for some clue. With Smith, one never knew.

"Our stepmother is being blackmailed."

"Heard that's been going around," Smith replied.

"Are you working another case?"

He didn't answer either way and Violet glanced at Victor who shook his head slightly. Victor didn't know any more than Vi.

"We'd like your help finding out who is doing it, and also, if possible, discovering if Harry Mathers is in London."

"That's the partner of your sister's dead fiancé?"

Considering their association with Smith came far after those events, Violet was shocked he was aware of them, but not all that surprised upon further consideration.

Vi took a deep breath and then summarized the events of the engagement to the elder Mr. Danvers, the younger Mr. Danvers kidnapping Isolde, and the financial crimes that eventually put Harry Mathers in jail.

"Not easy to break out of prison," Smith said. "I doubt the fellow did it without help."

"That was our assumption," Victor told Smith. "We need to find out who helped him and if either of them is connected to Lady Eleanor."

"I can delve into the prison." Smith lifted a brow and then glanced between them. "You might get a message from me if I get in and need help getting out, but I suspect I won't need it. I have, in my idle moments, planned several escapes from prison."

"Have you also planned how to get away with murder?" Violet demanded.

"Of course, I have. Haven't you?"

"I don't plan on murdering anyone," Violet said. "Why would I need to?"

"I don't plan to either, but we see so many people who've become killers who wouldn't have imagined doing so. For meddlers, like yourself, it's just a matter of time."

"I hardly think so," Violet snapped.

His ridiculously handsome face seemed to emphasize his scoff more than someone less beautiful. Violet scowled back at him, and he simply met her gaze. She finally shook it off.

"Fine, get it done however you need to do it. We need to know how Mathers got out of prison. I'm not sure how else we'll get the information we need without linking whoever helped him to Lady Eleanor. Or at least someone who could have known what Carlton Danvers knew to use against our stepmother."

"You know," Smith said thoughtfully, "your father seems like a person who might know more than his wife would think."

Victor cleared his throat but said nothing. Vi knew

her brother well enough to know that he also thought it might be possible that Father would have a pretty good idea of why Lady Eleanor was being harassed. The twins' gazes met and they had another one of their silent exchanges. Victor finally said, "I'll look into it."

~

VIOLET RAN her fingers along the edges of her letter from Jack and then went out to the auto. Holmes darted ahead, so she couldn't leave him behind. She had called for the auto on the off chance that she'd be able to engineer her way into Genevieve Bromley's home. Or perhaps instead she'd consider trying to visit Lottie Wilder and ensure that her affections were fixed. The chances were likely, Violet thought, that if Genevieve Bromley really thought she'd be able to marry Gerald, Vi would be able to acquire an invitation to her house without a problem.

But did Violet want to stick her oar in there? Genevieve Bromley was on the list of those who might be an enemy of Lady Eleanor. What exactly, Violet wondered, had her stepmother promised the wealthy Bromley daughter?

Before Violet decided which way to go, she read Jack's vague letter in the peace of the auto. Their letters had crossed paths, so he hadn't answered her latest questions, and any news from his end was as vague as she expected. The letter did, however, remind her that he was alive, she was in his thoughts, and they loved each other.

Lottie had left a note for Violet, inspiring Vi to dare something else instead. The note was nothing more than a thank you, but Violet would rather get to know Lottie better than deal with the lies Lady Eleanor had probably told Miss Bromley. Vi motored to the middle-class house where Lottie's family lived and knocked on the door. The woman who opened the door eyed Violet suspiciously.

"Hullo," Violet said brightly, ignoring the daggered glance she was sending Vi's way.

"A Carlyle?"

Violet nodded, wondering how the woman knew. The woman started to close the door, but Violet pushed her foot into place. "What happened?"

"My husband was called in early today for a special meeting with his superiors."

Violet took a slow breath in, despising her step-mother. "Have you heard from him?"

She shook her head. The freckles and the long dark hair matched Lottie. As did the large, slow tears.

"He works at the main branch?" Vi asked.

She nodded.

Violet spun on her heel, driven by her contempt for her stepmother. Mrs. Wilder followed. "What are you going to do?"

"My brother is going to marry your daughter, your husband is going to have a position, and my father is not behind this. The person who is will regret her choices."

"How?"

"Lady Eleanor is not the only force in the Carlyle family, and she is not the most powerful of us despite what she thinks."

"That's you?" Mrs. Wilder asked doubtfully

"No," Vi laughed. "Not at all, but I know them better than you, and I'm certain my father would find Lady

Eleanor's actions appalling." Violet crossed her fingers as she left the Wilder home. She very much hoped that the attitude Father had about Jack and his suitability would extend to Father's heir. Gerald, after all, was far more important than Vi. His wife would, therefore, be of far greater concern as well.

CHAPTER 8

*V*iolet approached the doors to the bank with her dog under her arm. She was wearing one of her more simple day dresses and only had a wedding ring on. Most of the signs of her status were hidden, but she knew her name would do the necessaries. She despised putting on the persona of a woman like Lady Eleanor, and the more Violet used it these days, the more Violet felt as though she were putting on a mask that no longer fit.

But for family? She'd do whatever she could. Violet bypassed the guard at the door, the banker who was ready to dart into play for the richest of customers, and walked directly to the manager's office. As she approached, the manager's secretary leapt to his feet, took in her snidely lifted brow, and then opened the office door with Violet's name on his lips.

"Lady Violet Carlyle-Wakefield, sir."

"I prefer Mrs. Wakefield," Violet answered, smiling

cheerily. She'd read the manager's name on the door and knew the man was called James Season. "Mr. Season, I understand that you have received some information regarding Mr. Wilder? He's one of your employees, I believe."

"Ah, he's currently on an unpaid leave, my lady," the manager said. "We understand that your family has strong feelings on the manner, but ah—"

"If by strong feelings you mean that my stepmother told you we wanted Mr. Wilder to be dismissed, you are incorrect."

The manager's mouth dropped open and he stammered, "She—she—was quite clear, my lady."

"I'm sure she was. Mr. Season, may I apologize that you have been sucked into a bit of a family squabble?"

His gaze widened.

"It's entirely unfair to you, but if you will change the unpaid leave to a paid leave and apologize to Mr. Wilder on behalf of myself, the future earl, Gerald Carlyle, my twin brother, Victor Carlyle, and—I believe —the earl, you'll see that this is all sorted out quite quickly."

Mr. Season paused and then confessed, "Mr. Wilder is currently working in our back office."

Violet smiled wickedly at Mr. Season. "I believe you were hoping that Lady Eleanor would turn her attention elsewhere and the good Mr. Wilder would not need to be dismissed."

"Mr. Wilder is highly valued."

"Wonderful. I'll handle Lady Eleanor."

James Season glanced at his closed office door and then back to Violet. "And if you cannot?"

She struggled through what she could reveal and then said, "I believe that Lady Eleanor may have warned you that the earl will pull his funds from the bank if you do not do as she wishes."

He cleared his throat but didn't reply, which was answer enough. He no doubt feared that Lady Eleanor would not only urge the earl to pull his funds, she might encourage others to withdraw their money from the bank too. Mr. Season was a businessman. As such, he would have to protect the bank's interest, even at the cost of a valued employee.

"That is a threat that can go both ways," Violet told him, hating herself for adding to the threat he faced.

Mr. Season's eyes widened. He nodded silently.

Violet grimaced, unable to keep up the pretense. "I apologize for strong-arming you, Mr. Season. It was unkind of me and quite out of how I should wish to behave. The most I can say for myself is that I didn't want to be part of this, but I felt that Mr. Wilder deserved not just the enmity of my family but also the defense. Please forgive me."

Mr. Season nodded again with relief. Violet smiled at him, and it was an apologetic one. She left the bank, at least satisfied that Mr. Wilder's position was not immediately at risk. She walked back to her auto and sat behind the wheel with Holmes in her lap. She held him like a baby and rubbed his belly while he gazed adoringly at her.

"You make me feel better about myself, Holmesy. Who's a good boy? Who's a good, sweet boy?" Violet frowned down at her dog, feeling fraudulent, and then started the auto again. She wanted nothing more than to go back to her house, curl up with an Arthur Conan Doyle novel and a cup of cocoa. She wanted to shed the persona she'd put on. It was important, she told herself, to remember that being the daughter of an earl did not make her more important.

There was a tap on her window and Vi gasped before she rolled the window down. There was no question that the person knocking on the door was Lottie's father. He had the same blue eyes and many freckles, but his hair was a medium reddish brown.

"Mrs. Wakefield?"

Violet nodded, letting Holmes go. The dog stuck his head out the window, tail wagging frantically, and barked at Lottie's father.

"Mr. Wilder?" Violet returned.

He nodded and swallowed thickly. "I wanted to thank you."

"You're welcome." Her voice was gentle and kind. "I'd like to apologize for my family."

He paused and Violet wondered if she'd offended him before he said, "I wasn't expecting that."

"I realize I put on my internal tiara and made veiled threats in response to my stepmother's, but I'd like to not be that person."

"Your stepmother's threats weren't veiled."

Violet pressed her lips together to prevent a fervent curse. "My brother loves your daughter."

"Does he, really?"

"I promise that he does."

"I realize you just did me a favor," he shot back

respectfully, "but my daughter is my priority. I don't think that a relationship with your brother is what is best for her, or for our family."

"You have every reason to despise my stepmother and have concerns about my brother. The aristocracy is, in general, a bunch of useless, spoiled blights. In my experience. But Gerald is a good man who would devote himself to your daughter's happiness."

Mr. Wilder cleared his throat, expression perfectly controlled.

Violet laughed. "You have the same control over your expression as my friend, Hargreaves." She reached out and took Mr. Wilder's hand as she added, "Why don't you give Gerald a chance?"

Mr. Wilder didn't react and Violet tried for woebegone eyes. He was clearly a man who actually parented his daughters because he was unmoved. "It's not best for her or our family. It'll end, and she'll find someone who is a better match."

Violet bit down on her bottom lip and she made another attempt. "My family tried to tell me who to marry. It didn't work."

Mr. Wilder eyed Violet sternly. "Lottie is a good girl."

"Gerald is a good man."

"I'm sure he is, but that doesn't make him the right man for my daughter."

Why did anyone want to tell another so blithely and arrogantly who to marry? Violet nodded to Mr. Wilder, knowing she wouldn't get any further at the moment. "I fear we'll never agree on certain matters, Mr. Wilder. Thank you for your time."

She left him and motored to her house. She couldn't

help but compare her own marriage to Jack, Isolde's engagement to Danvers, and Lottie being pulled away from Gerald. When Violet reached her home, she stopped the auto but didn't immediately get out.

Vi's mood would be so much better if she hadn't just spoken to Mr. Wilder. How difficult would it be to let Charlotte Wilder just live her own life? Lady Eleanor was overt with her manipulating, but how much worse was it when it was a good and kind father?

Holmes huffed at Vi and then licked Violet's chin. "Thank you, baby."

Violet rubbed her chin across the top of his head before stepping out of the auto. She found Victor inside the house waiting for her return.

"I found Father," Victor told her. "He's come back."

"I found Lottie's father. Lady Eleanor pulled her stunt. I tried to counteract it, but he's still decided that his good little girl cannot marry Gerald."

Victor's expression made Violet feel better. He led her to a Chesterfield and then crossed to the bar and made her a drink. It was orange and blackberry and sweet, and she loved it, but it didn't make her feel better.

Violet leaned her head against Victor's shoulder when he sat next to her, wrapping an arm around her shoulders. "Do you think that Lottie will let her father win?"

Victor wound their fingers together. "Do you remember when we used to be jealous of the others? It always seemed that they got it better. We never understood how great Aunt Agatha was until later."

"It felt like we were thrown away," Violet agreed.

"What would we have done if Father had actually raised us and then tried to convince us to not marry Kate or Jack? I know Lady Eleanor did, but what if it were Aunt Agatha?"

"We'd have listened," Violet said in a hushed tone.

"I'd have listened for certain." Victor sighed. "I'd have been wrong, but I don't think Aunt Agatha would have done that to us."

"She was special," Violet said. "It makes me sad to think that Lottie doesn't have someone who would do the same for her. I wouldn't be so upset, I guess, if Gerald wasn't a worthy man. Lottie would be lucky to marry him. She'd be lucky to be his priority. She'd be lucky—"

Victor pressed a kiss on the top of her head. "I know, Vi. I know. I'm blue too." He squeezed her fingers.

"I want Jack."

"I want to talk to Lottie, but I'm not sure it would have any effect."

"Do you remember what you said? That she made Gerald beg. And he did."

Victor laughed suddenly and sipped his drink. "It was a beautiful moment."

They both needed something other to focus on. "Let's go see Ginny," Violet told him.

CHAPTER 9

"There she is," Violet said, pointing towards a tree. A thick woolen blanket lay under it and on the blanket in a school girl's uniform lay Ginny Carlyle. Half-adopted, half-ward, all theirs and not in class.

"I knew it," Victor crowed and then paused. "Oh, I suppose I'm not supposed to crow. Look at her! Not in class."

"Is that Geoffrey?" Violet demanded. "That's Geoffrey! That—what—"

"What's that blighter doing here?"

"Oh bloody hell," Violet gasped, "look at that!" Vi's mouth dropped open as she watched her wartish younger brother tuck back Ginny's hair and press a kiss on her forehead. Vi hurried towards the twosome and her gasp of rage had them springing apart.

"Is this some kind of terrible joke?"

Ginny leapt to her feet while Geoffrey followed,

putting himself in front of Ginny. Vi glanced at Victor, who quirked a brow. "Are you protecting her from us?"

"I know you're angry," Geoffrey said, "but you don't need to look at her like that. It's the modern day, Vi. I—we—we can be together if we want to."

Violet was utterly flabbergasted. She gaped at Victor, who was fighting a grin.

"I know that there are expectations," Victor said, "but Ginny is a Carlyle now. She's one of us. We can't expect her not to follow her own will."

Violet snapped her mouth closed, turning her gaze to Ginny.

"I'm sorry," Ginny said precisely. Her eyes were downturned, and she was blushing deeply.

"For what?"

"For...for thinking that we could be together." Her gaze moved to Geoffrey and then back to her feet. Violet knew society would look with disapproval if Geoffrey and Ginny, both Carlyles, were together, no matter that they weren't truly related.

"We don't care about that," Victor told Ginny gently and it was true. Society's opinion had never been important to the twins. "You are too young though."

"And supposed to be in school," Violet added, calming. "He's not good enough for you."

"Hey!" Geoffrey said.

"He's wartish," Victor agreed. "Definitely not good enough for you."

"I've been better," Geoffrey snapped. "I'm trying."

"You're brilliant," Violet told Ginny, "and too young."

"We love each other," Geoffrey said flatly.

"Too. Young," Violet repeated precisely. "Bloody hell.

You both need to finish school."

"So if we weren't too young, you wouldn't object." Ginny's expression said exactly where she expected the problem lay—with herself.

"We're fleeing the idiocy of parents who interfere with love stories. We aren't ever going to do that to you, Ginny." Violet reached out, and it was her turn to tuck Ginny's hair behind her ear and then pulled her close. "We love you, Ginny Carlyle."

Ginny let out a shaky sob and then Violet looked up at Geoffrey and pulled him close too. "We love you too, Geoffrey."

It was Geoffrey who eyes reddened with tears that time, but he didn't let one go. He did, however, hug her back, tightly.

Violet squeezed him and let him go. She kept Ginny close and pressed another kiss to Ginny's forehead. "You thought you weren't good enough? That we'd choose Geoffrey over you?"

Ginny nodded, another tear falling.

"You are good enough for anyone. And we are not the Capulets and the Montagues." Violet ignored the way the two smiled adoringly at each other. "Listen to me," Violet told them both seriously. "You are too young. But more importantly, you need to be fully and completely sure before you let something like this come out. Your mother is terrifying."

"I know," Geoffrey said, avoiding their gazes.

"Is this why you wanted to go to school here?" Victor asked Ginny. He didn't look upset but more delighted at their cleverness.

Violet shot him a nasty look but he ignored her.

"Not entirely," Ginny said.

"I wanted her to go to school closer to me," Geoffrey said. "But this is a good school, and they're much nicer to her here. They care less about where you're from and more about what you know."

Violet took a deep breath in and then asked, "Are you studying as well?"

"Today was stuff I already knew," Ginny said. "I don't miss classes where I would be learning new things."

"And you?" Victor demanded of Geoffrey.

"Poetry," Geoffrey muttered. "Ginny convinced me to try harder at school, but I flat out refused to try for poetry. We meet here on the days when I have poetry and Ginny already knows the stuff in her lecture."

"Is she having a good effect on him?" Victor asked Violet, but it was Geoffrey who answered.

"She's too stubborn for me to have a bad effect on her."

Violet laughed and then scowled at him. "This goes on hiatus."

Geoffrey scowled in return, shaking his head belligerently.

"You can be best friends. You can long for one another. You can write love letters, but if you do anything else--any touching, any other things—"

"You'll what?" Geoffrey demanded.

"Well, we can punish you without punishing Ginny simply by allowing Lady Eleanor to know."

Geoffrey's face paled.

"Your mother is a monster," Violet told him flatly. "Or rather, I am not her biggest fan."

"I know," he said. "I know." It was Geoffrey who eyed

his feet. "She's not a monster, but she's...difficult. She won't like this." He took Ginny's hand and squeezed it tightly.

"So wait," Violet told him. "If you love Ginny—"

"I do," he swore.

"Your mother will make her miserable when she learns. The only avenue of peace is to keep your feelings silent and make sure they last the test of time. You can't act on your feelings now anyway. You both know you're too young."

Violet shook her head at the couple who had already stepped back together, edging close like magnets that were drawn to each other, clinging to the other's hand as if it were a life raft and their ship was going down.

"Bloody hell," Victor muttered. "Star-crossed."

"No," Violet snapped. "With any luck, we could just lie to her. Make her think they're best friends like us."

"She's not stupid."

"She is blind to the vagaries of Geoffrey. They might get away with anything as long as Geoffrey tells her what she wants to hear. What do you know about your mother's latest issues?" She purposefully changed the subject sharply.

Geoffrey shifted from foot to foot, not answering at once. Wart though he might be, he was also a Carlyle and clever.

"I—"

"It's important, Geoffrey," Violet told him.

"I don't know anything specific. You know she treats me like I'm in short pants and need her handling my leading strings."

Geoffrey had flushed but Violet did not believe it was

from embarrassment. There was something he knew.

"Do you know why Isolde was engaged to Danvers?" she pressed.

Geoffrey surprised her by nodding.

"Why?"

"I can't tell you."

"How did you find out?"

"I lurk," he said.

"He does," Ginny added, but Violet already knew that. "You can tell them," she said quietly to Geoffrey.

"You know?" Violet was shocked. Apparently so was Victor, as his jaw dropped.

Ginny winced, which was all the answer Violet needed.

"What is it?"

"I can't tell you," Ginny said. "It's Geoffrey's to tell."

Violet studied Geoffrey. He was tan now, she realized. He looked better. The white-blonde of his hair wasn't so stark against cheeks that were healthier with glowing skin. His eyes were bright.

"You look good," Violet told him. "I'm happy to see you looking so healthy."

Geoffrey shook his head at Violet's compliment. "Being nice to me won't change things. You two don't ever try to be nice to me. I can't trust you with my mother's secrets."

Violet glanced at Ginny, but her gaze was fixated on Geoffrey, not Vi. She turned to Victor who looked almost as guilty as Violet felt.

"We're the warts," Victor said with a sigh. "Your mother is being blackmailed," he confessed.

Geoffrey swallowed thickly and shifted, but he didn't

speak up.

"We're trying to help her."

"Of course you are," Geoffrey said sarcastically.

Violet's gaze was fixed on the two clutching each other's hands as though no one would come between them. Geoffrey's lip was quivering slightly and his skin had paled somewhat under his tan. He wouldn't look at Violet or Victor while Ginny was watching him with such care and concern.

Violet was struck by realization.

"It's all right," Violet told him. "You don't have to tell us." He looked at her in confusion. "You know. We're family," Vi said. "No matter what."

He flushed brilliantly but he didn't speak. Victor stared at Violet and he saw something in her expression that took him aback.

Violet felt as if her whole life was being rewritten in her head. She nibbled on her bottom lip and then she said to Geoffrey. "It makes sense that your mother would expect things would be all right for Isolde by marrying Danvers. They were for her after all."

Geoffrey flushed a shocking red, his ears were so dark they were almost purple, but he didn't say anything.

"It's harder to be empathetic about things we've experienced ourselves, you know. It's like our rough times callous us to things others face that we've gone through and survived."

"What are you saying, Vi?" Victor asked.

"I'm saying that Lady Eleanor didn't necessarily want to marry Father. They aren't that fond of each other. She's not really a monster as much as I don't care for her. But it would make sense that she'd never find the ability to love us, her stepchildren, if she'd been pressured into leaving behind a real love for the earl."

Geoffrey cleared his throat, but Violet wasn't paying attention to his face. Her gaze was fixed on the clutching hands of Geoffrey and Ginny. Ginny's thumb was rubbing over the back of his hand. The comforting move cemented for Violet that she was on the right track.

"Your mother favors you over Isolde because you are the son of the man she loved." Violet said it as though commenting on the weather, not dropping a bomb in the middle of all their lives.

Geoffrey shook his head frantically, but Ginny's gaze was so full of love and empathy that Violet felt certain that she was right.

"That's a secret worth paying for," Violet told Victor, who was blinking rapidly in astonishment.

"Father—"

Vi nodded. She had no idea what Father would do with the information. It was hardly the first time that someone like Father had a cuckoo in his nest, and given that there was little chance Geoffrey could inherit, Father might know and decide to let it go.

"We won't tell him," Violet told Geoffrey.

"Violet, how did you guess?" Victor demanded.

"I was always making excuses for why Lady Eleanor favored Geoffrey over Isolde. His chances to inherit are remarkably slim. She'd naturally want the best for both her children, but it always seemed as though Isolde were an afterthought while she spoiled Geoffrey to no end. It makes sense if I put myself in her position. What possible reason would I have for so clearly favoring one child? It was always clear she did, you know, even from the time you were little. She absolutely doted on Geoffrey as an infant. But she would, of course, if he were the child of the man she loved."

Both Victor and Violet faced Geoffrey. He finally slumped in defeat, admitting the truth with his posture if not with words.

Violet reached out and cupped Geoffrey's chin. "I don't care that we aren't related. Not any more than I care that Gerald is my half-brother or that Ginny wasn't born a Carlyle."

"I'm a bastard, Vi," Geoffrey hissed, glancing around. "It's why my mother has been paying the blackmailer and why Isolde almost paid with her future."

"How did Mr. Danvers know?" Violet asked. "I can't imagine that your mother would have announced it."

"I don't have any idea."

"How did you find out?"

Geoffrey's blush couldn't have been brighter, but he seemed to be calming down. "I went through her things. I found love letters between her and my real father."

"Who is your father?"

Geoffrey didn't answer.

"Does he know about you?"

Geoffrey nodded, swallowed harshly, and said hoarsely, "He looks in on me sometimes. I see him at a game or in one of those debates I lose every time. I'm not sure he has any reason to be proud of me."

Violet had to wonder if Geoffrey's father were the blackmailer. He knew the secret. He had to be a suspect, but Violet couldn't push at Geoffrey for the name. He was too fragile. She had to wonder, however, if Lady Eleanor's love letters were still around.

CHAPTER 10

*V*iolet found Gerald in his rooms at their father's house the next morning. He was seated at his desk in his private office, drinking coffee and reading his paper.

"Do you always hide in here?" she asked.

"Yes," he said unapologetically. "Even before the whole Lottie mess."

"Have you heard from her?"

He eyed Violet, examining her face. "I appreciate that you tried to help me." He sounded exhausted. He had bags under his eyes and the food that had been placed before him had been left untouched. "I fear that your visit to the bank wasn't enough. Lottie's parents didn't know about how things were before then. How serious things were between us. When Eleanor intervened in Mr. Wilder's work, they realized the truth of our relationship. Now—" Gerald shook his head, seeming defeated.

"Did Lottie change her mind?"

He shook his head and then in a near-broken voice, he said, "She says she has to think. She says her father loves her and he seems convinced that she'll eventually be happier with someone else. He told her people fall in and out of love and that losing me now will be for her long-term good."

Violet winced and she sat down across from him. "What are you going to do?"

"I don't know," Gerald admitted. "I can't make her choose me. I just want to be first to one person, Vi. Her."

"That's what she needs to do," Violet told him. "I suppose if Victor had been determined in objections over my relationship with Jack—especially in the early days— I'd have seriously considered ending things."

"But now you wouldn't."

Violet shook her head. "Even if Jack and Victor were fixated on hating each other, I would be tortured but I would choose Jack over Victor. Happily for me, the two most important people in my life work hard on being friends."

Gerald looked at Violet for a while. "What is it about you, Vi, that makes me want to tell you all my woes?"

"It's my eyes," Violet told him, "and you know you can trust me. You know me."

Gerald leaned forward. "What would you do, Violet?"

She paused, twirling her hair around her finger as she considered. "I would confess my love and ask him to choose me."

"I did that," Gerald said hoarsely. "I begged. Tears in my eyes. Hand on my heart. She said she needed time."

"Then all you can do is give her time."

Gerald scoffed and put his hands over his face.

"Thank you for saving her father's position, Vi. I've talked to Father. He's going to speak with Eleanor and also with the bank manager. The Wilder family won't go hungry and homeless because I dared to love."

Violet didn't have anything else to say. She hurt for her brother. Both Gerald and Geoffrey for that matter. Why was their family so broken over their different definitions of status?

Vi wanted to talk to Father concerning what she'd learned about Geoffrey, but she could understand her little brother's fears, and she wasn't going to be the one who told Father that Geoffrey wasn't his son. Not if it would ruin their relationship. Geoffrey had his birth father poking around and still wanted the man who raised him.

Violet rubbed her temple. "Where's Lady Eleanor?"

"I avoid her, so I don't know."

"Could you find out if she's left the house and when she'll be back?"

Gerald hesitated, clearly debating between his despise for Lady Eleanor and his desire to help Violet, and then rang the bell for the servants. "Why do you want to know? And I assume you want coffee?"

"Do you have Turkish coffee?"

Gerald shook his head.

"Then tea is fine. I'm going to search her room and discover her secrets."

Gerald snorted, entirely unbothered by Violet's confession. They waited until the housemaid arrived. Gerald ordered tea for Violet and then asked, "Oh Maggie, is my stepmother in the house?"

Maggie shook her head. "I believe she left this morning."

"Do we know when she'll be back?"

"She said she'd be home in time for tea."

"The earl is also gone, isn't he?" Violet asked.

The maid glanced at Violet. "He went to his club, Lady Violet."

"Thank you, Maggie," Gerald answered and then he turned his gaze to Violet. "What are you up to?"

"Lady Eleanor hasn't told me anything about who is blackmailing her. She's never going to," Violet said. "It's obvious that I'll have to discover this for myself."

"I'm not that interested in helping her, Vi. I have been fighting every moment not to wring her neck."

Violet could understand those feelings. She felt them herself. "She doesn't exist in a vacuum."

Gerald sighed. "Like I said, I want to strangle her. As much as I want to help you get out of your promise to her, Violet, I can't help Eleanor. Not right now. I don't know what to do with myself. I'm seething with hatred and fear."

"You should buy a house," Violet told him. "Get a dog. You should write Lottie love letters and send her the address to the house. Paint her a picture of what your life could be like. Make sure you include her family in it."

"I don't know if I can do that."

"Her parents love her, Gerald. Help her know that the wall between her and them won't be built by you."

Gerald rubbed his brow. "A house, huh?"

"There's one on the street where Victor and I live, you know. It's not quite so overtly arrogant as this neighborhood, but perhaps she'd be more comfortable with quite a bit of distance between herself and Lady Eleanor's cronies."

Violet left Gerald in his office and made her way through her father's house. She had very rarely stayed there despite being one of the earl's children. It mattered less and less as she grew in wisdom.

Violet took the servants' stairs from Gerald's wing of the house to Lady Eleanor's bedroom. The room was lace-covered in shades of pink and magenta. Luxurious beyond what was necessary and nothing like what Violet's mother had kept when it had been her room.

Violet had a creeping sense of sympathy for Lady Eleanor. She had married for money while she was in love with another man. Violet both hurt for her step-mother and thought she was an idiot for choosing the mansion and money over love.

What did Violet know, however? She had no idea what situation had driven her stepmother to marry the earl. She closed the door behind her and crossed to Lady Eleanor's desk. She opened and closed drawers, searching for the packet of letters that Geoffrey described.

Love letters, blackmail letters, would they be together? Violet worked quickly and silently, searching until a flash of memory struck her. It was a moment in her past, snuggled on her own mother's lap. Violet closed her eyes, seeking for it. Mother had been kneeling on the ground near the window, looking out into the back garden and then opened a window seat and reached in, pulling out a doll.

Vi couldn't remember her own reaction to the doll, but she slowly crossed the bedroom floor and lifted the window seat. At the bottom of the enclosed space, Violet found an old hatbox. She pulled it out and opened it. It was full of letters. Violet unfolded one of the newest and found a letter signed by Genevieve Bromley. Vi folded it and then opened another, finding a note from the blackmailer.

Lady E,

Secrets like yours cost more than you've paid. £500.00 by the fifteenth. Same place.

Yours.

Violet closed the box to take back with her to Gerald's rooms. The moment she shut the bedroom door she heard, "Vi?"

Violet turned and faced her father. His gaze landed on her face, moved to the box, and then back to her face.

"I thought you were at your club," she told him, knowing he had guessed that she'd been going through Lady Eleanor's things.

"What are you doing?"

"Helping," Violet said evenly. Helping deal with the blackmail because Lady Eleanor didn't feel as though she could go to her husband, who was certainly one of the most powerful men in England when he chose to be, but of course, she couldn't say all of that.

His gaze was still on the box and then he slowly asked, "What do you know?"

Violet stepped closer to him, to see his gaze more clearly. "What do you know?"

"I'm not stupid, Violet. I have a fairly good idea of my life's particulars."

"All of them?"

"Who told you?" he asked wearily.

"Geoffrey," Violet answered, watching carefully. "Geoffrey figured it out. He knows."

Father closed his eyes, but there was no other reaction. "How long has he known?"

"I don't know. He's afraid we won't want him anymore."

Father cursed. "I chose to make him mine a long time ago, Violet. I knew before he was even born that I wasn't the father."

Violet started but she recovered quickly. "Lady Eleanor has been blackmailed over this. It was one of the reasons why she pushed Isolde at Danvers."

Her father seemed entirely unmoved, but she doubted it was the case. "She's paying blackmail?"

Violet nodded. "She thinks it's Harry Mathers because he was partners with Danvers."

"Danvers wasn't the man she threw over for the title. How did he know about Ellie's lover?" The casual use of her stepmother's name was so foreign to Violet she started. How was it possible that Lady Eleanor was an Ellie to anyone, let alone Vi's father? The realization that there were decades of relationship and feeling that Violet knew very little about was as shocking as the name itself.

"I don't know."

"She's been paying blackmail for how long?"

"I don't know."

Father cursed and then said, "You shouldn't take those. She likes to read them whenever she's angry with me. She'll know they're gone."

Violet tucked the box under her arm and tilted her head at her father. "Maybe because of comments like that one. However, I don't really care if she knows I took them."

"Are you endeavoring to advise me in my marriage?"

"Father," Violet said quietly, "you've made quite a mess of your marriage all by yourself." After a moment's reflection, she added, "Perhaps you and Lady Eleanor have done that together. But it's still a mess."

"Your marriage is early days yet, Violet. The pain builds off of little cuts over years and years. Thicker, stronger, more calloused until there is nothing left but resignation."

Violet shook her head and then said, "You need to talk to Geoffrey, Father."

He didn't say anything, so Violet left him to it. As she walked towards the front of the house, she could hear him follow, but he didn't say anything until she reached the bottom of the stairs.

"I'll talk to him, Violet."

She glanced back at him.

"I need to apologize to you as well."

She blinked in surprise.

"I left you to suffer those pranks while I tried to work out stopping them without telling you. I hadn't realized how bothered you were. I—"

"I couldn't sleep in my own house, Father. That brat had a body dug up and dumped at my party."

"I know." He sounded sick. "I was angry when you sidestepped what I wanted. I should have put you first, Vi."

"You chose to keep things even-keeled with your friends over helping me."

"I did."

Violet shifted the hat box as she turned to face him. "I already feel like the child you wanted least. It didn't help, Father."

He started to reply, but Violet held up a hand.

"If being Ginny's guardian has taught me anything, it's that parents have no idea what they're doing. We make mistakes. We guess blindly."

Her father's look of relief made Violet feel as though he was as twisted up as she was. "I do love you, Violet."

"I believe you." Violet fought back the rush of tears. She abruptly changed the subject. "This thing is a mess, Father. Harry Mathers has escaped prison. He wants revenge on Danvers."

"Danvers is dead."

"Isolde isn't."

Father's expression told Violet that he didn't truly know the particulars of what had been happening with his wife. Her genial father looked dangerous all of the sudden. He hadn't been bothered by the lost money, but the threat to his daughter had him shifting just as Victor did when he was feeling protective. Spaniel to lion.

"Victor telegrammed Tomas."

"Of course he did. Your aunt did a good job teaching you two to look after each other and those you love."

"She did," Violet agreed. There was a little girl inside of her who still felt abandoned and unwanted, but the woman knew how lucky she had been to have her life be the way it was. Aunt Agatha had loved, raised, taught, and protected the twins. Everything that was good about the twins had been uncovered and nurtured by Aunt Agatha.

"I love you, Violet. I always have. I failed you. I'm failing Geoffrey. I've even failed Gerald. He's a mess, too."

Violet looked around her. Everywhere she looked was utterly luxurious, but there was so much unnecessary suffering in their family. It was ridiculous that they were so unhappy when they had everything.

"We all fail, Father," Violet told him. "We have to keep trying."

"Will you give me another chance then?"

"If I wasn't willing to do that, I wouldn't have responded to Lady Eleanor's summons. We might be a broken little family, but we are a family, aren't we?"

"That we are."

"I love you. I'm here because that hasn't changed." She examined his face as she said, "You're including Geoffrey?" There was a piece of her that knew if he gave her the wrong answer things would never be the same.

"Of course," Father said without delay, and Violet instantly forgave him for what had happened between them.

She stepped towards him and kissed his cheek. "Let's fix this then."

He nodded.

"Your job is Geoffrey."

Father winced, but he said, "It's overdue."

CHAPTER 11

*V*iolet paced the parlor, staring at the list of names. The thing about those names was that they were nonsense. Lady Eleanor had given them to Violet and then shoved harder on Harry Mathers. Why? Harry Mathers had been a knowing contributor to the fraud associated with Danvers. He'd been put in prison with dark men and had gone mad. Maybe he'd always been mad. The sort of quid pro quo negotiation that ruined people and destroyed their lives. Maybe the madness had become emphasized when he had endless time to think about it.

"Violet?"

She looked up to see the concerned gaze of her twin. The hatbox of letters was open on the couch where Violet had been sitting, and she was pacing to outrace the letters. How true were they? How much of that longing in Lady Eleanor's letters was real? How much of it was romantic? Was she nurturing the love because it gave her something to focus on when she realized that luxury wasn't all it seemed from the outside?

"They were like Denny and Lila," Violet told him. "Eleanor and Mitchell. They were raised together in the same little village. Their families were extremely close. Up until she met Father, everyone assumed she'd marry him. Just like Denny and Lila."

"But Denny and Lila really were devoted," Victor said without sympathy. "Denny and Lila weren't wealthy at first. Lila is pretty enough she could have snapped up one of the wealthier lads. Instead, she married Denny, and they struggled just like you and I struggled. Sardines and eggs, darling. Worth it to save ourselves from the choice Eleanor made."

Violet rubbed her hand over her chin as she paced. "He never married."

"So he loved her more than she loved him."

"Or, the broken trust between them destroyed his ability to trust anyone at all." Violet glanced at Victor and said, "What if you dropped in on Kate and found she was with a lover instead of her mother."

Victor looked as though he'd been punched in the kidney. "Don't say such things."

"You'd be ruined. Would you ever love or trust another woman again?"

Victor hadn't lost his sick look as he shook his head. "Probably not."

"I want to meet Geoffrey's birth father," Violet told Victor. "I want to talk to him, but I'm afraid that he won't talk to us."

"Father went to visit Geoffrey. He said he's bringing both Geoffrey and Ginny home for a bit."

"Do you think Geoffrey will be all right? I'm so worried about him. I don't know that Father—I don't know if I trust him to make everything well with Geoffrey. He doesn't have the best history of doing right by his children."

"Who knows, Vi? Father is who he is. He knew that Geoffrey wasn't his and never let it bother him. Maybe all Geoffrey needs to know is that Father always loved him. My question is about Geoffrey's other father. What do we call him? Real father feels wrong."

"I don't know." Violet lifted a brow. "You aren't suggesting that we ask Geoffrey to meet his natural father for this case, are you?"

Victor scoffed and then added, "I'm suggesting we lie to the man. What if we call him the first father?"

"Let's just use his name." Violet nibbled on her bottom lip as she went back to pacing. "It's a nasty move to ask the man here as though Geoffrey will be here."

"So is blackmailing someone."

"There's no reason to believe that it is him who is blackmailing her. Why would he look in on Geoffrey and then ruin him?"

"I'm just saying if Father could do the math to realize Geoffrey isn't his, this fellow could have done the math to realize who actually fathered him. The man would have known the secret," Victor said and then considered. "He obviously cares about Geoffrey, Vi. If he's looking in on him, he cares enough to make sure Geoffrey is all right. So it wouldn't make sense for him to be the blackmailer."

"I'll write him a letter," Violet told Victor. "Here's hoping he doesn't murder us when he realizes we were playing with his heart."

Victor stood. "I can't imagine someone else raising my girls, Vi. Not when I could only look on from a distance."

Violet nodded and went back to pacing. She glanced at Victor as she did and watched him shift in his seat. The sick look hadn't left his face, and she imagined there was a matching one on her face. Why were they doing something so heartless when they could imagine the pain so easily? Why were they allowing themselves to become monsters to benefit Lady Eleanor?

Vi's gaze fell on the letters that she'd stolen. As tragic as those letters were, Violet simply didn't feel all that sorry for Eleanor. It wasn't as if she was beaten until she changed her mind. It wasn't as if someone compelled her either way to leave behind her love and marry the earl.

The letters made it clear that Eleanor chose to marry the earl. She wanted to be a countess, she wanted the mansions, the parties, the excess of money. She wanted what the earl could offer, and the cost—the man she'd always loved—hadn't been too much to bear. It seemed that their early parting hadn't lasted. What had happened, Violet wondered, to bring the former lovers back together? Happenstance or deliberate reunion?

If it were Jack, Violet would have been destroyed. Somehow, however, Violet wasn't sure it was possible that her father had ever loved Lady Eleanor as much as Mitchell Fitzhugh had.

Violet fiddled with her ring again. The pacing wasn't

helping. What she wanted, what she needed, was to escape those letters and this situation.

"Have you heard from Smith?" Victor asked. She could feel his gaze on her and knew there was worry in it.

Violet shook her head and then crossed to the bell, ringing it. Beatrice worked in an office in Vi's house. Maybe Beatrice could get him to answer given she found him stalking her like a lion far too often.

Vi asked, still pacing, "Did you read the letters?"

Victor shook his head.

She crossed to the chalkboard and erased it. As she worked, she felt as though her skin were crawling. She shivered. "I don't like this case. I both have and don't have sympathy. I don't like what we're uncovering and most of all, I hate that the secrets are ours now."

"It'll be better in the end, Vi. For Geoffrey at least. He's been worried for who knows how long that we'd abandon him. Now he'll know that we won't."

Violet wrote on the top of the chalkboard:
WHAT WE KNOW

- Lady E is being blackmailed with an old secret.
- Algernon is being blackmailed.
- Someone helped Mathers escape prison

Violet sighed as she tossed the chalk down. "These things should be entirely disconnected. Algie and Eleanor? I bet they have never been in the same room unless we were there."

"There's us, though, Violet. We're that intersecting point."

"But we know we aren't doing this and neither of us know something that Algie might actually pay money over. He's been in many a scrape before and never felt the need to hide it so distinctly that he'd pay money to do so."

Victor crossed to Violet and picked up the chalk from where it had bounced from the ledge to the carpet. Next to Violet's list, he drew three intersecting lines, an incomplete starburst. The lines were crossing like an X with an extra line, and there was but one point of intersection between them all.

"There can't be a multitude of converging points, Vi. Whoever helped Mathers escape prison has to be the same person who is blackmailing Algie and our stepmother."

"Why?"

"As big as London is, her circle is small. Our circle is small. This is the same person. If these lines are threads, we just need to tug one and it'll all come unraveling. The truth of the matter is that Algie's secrets are there for anyone with a little wit and the ability to pay attention, but Eleanor's aren't. And Mathers? That makes the smallest amount of sense."

That was true, Violet thought. Their cousin had been half-blackmailed so often that it was old hat for him. Violet added another line to the starburst, putting Carlton Danvers name on it. The idea blossomed in her head and she darted from the parlor, running up the stairs. She shared her bedroom with Jack, but the typical lady-of-the-house room was set up for Vi as well. It was where she wrote when she couldn't sleep. The room held her writing desk, her clothes, and her bookshelf full of journals.

Violet dropped to her knees next to the now locking bookshelf, unlocked it, and opened volume after volume until she found the one that was from the timeframe when Carlton Danvers died.

Back then, Violet hadn't used chalkboards. She'd used her journal to gather her thoughts about the murders she'd seen along with her thoughts about Jack, her worries over Isolde—anything that had been bothering Violet had been written in those pages. She flipped through the pages until she found the list of suspects that she'd made. They were the people who were involved enough in Danvers's life to be possible killers.

Violet carried the list downstairs, her mind racing. Next to Victor's starburst, Violet wrote down the list of suspects from back then. They were:

Helen Mathers

Harry Mathers

Markus Kennington

Norman Kennington

Mr. Gulliver

Mr. Higgins

Hugo Danvers

Henry Carlyle

Victor came to stand next to Violet as they both looked over the names. There were no overlaps between the list of enemies of Lady Eleanor and the suspects of killing Carlton Danvers.

Victor took the chalk from Violet and added, "Anna Mathers."

"We need to talk to the Mathers sisters," Victor told Violet, watching her carefully.

"Anna is not blackmailing Eleanor," Violet said flatly. "She's barely younger than Ginny. And neither is Helen. They're good girls. Young ladies, I mean."

"It makes sense that Danvers's lover, Helen, knew about or found the blackmail that Danvers was conducting. Especially since she would have had access to both her father's papers and her lover's papers. And, if anyone would want Mathers out of prison, surely it would be his daughter."

"Helen and Anna are doing well! Just because they would want him out of prison doesn't mean that they'd have the first idea about how to get him out of prison."

"I know you care about them." Victor's patient voice infuriated Violet and she turned, punching him in the arm. "Hey!"

"It isn't Helen or Anna Mathers."

"I know you like Helen," Victor started again. "But look." He pointed to the starburst and tapped the black-mail line he'd created for Lady Eleanor and the Mathers prison line.

Violet stared, mouth firm, until he sighed.

"We could at least ask Algie and Clara if they know Helen Mathers. She could be an intersecting point, Violet. Check in on her. I know you've been writing to her for years. Go visit her and see how she is and—"

"And say what?" Violet shot back. "Hello again, Helen. I know I've supported and encouraged you for years, but I was wondering if you've decided that doesn't matter anymore and you thought it would be a good idea to blackmail my stepmother."

"Helen has to know you don't care for Lady Eleanor."

"She also certainly knows I care about Geoffrey and Isolde."

"Just talk to her," Victor insisted and Violet closed her eyes.

As much as Violet didn't want to do it, Victor—damn him—was right.

CHAPTER 12

*H*elen Mathers looked good. There was a brightness to her eyes that made Violet wonder if she'd seen her father and then immediately feel guilty for wondering such a thing.

"Vi!"

Violet pressed cheeks with Helen and squeezed a little tightly when they hugged.

"Anna is going to be so sad that you visited when she was at school. Are you up for a surprise visit? Or just here for shopping and clubs?"

Violet swallowed thickly and examined Helen again. She was wearing a maroon dress that flattered her trim figure. Any sign that Helen had given birth to Carlton Danvers's baby was gone. Violet wondered if Helen ever thought about the baby she'd given up.

"I was just thinking about you," Helen said. "You told me it would get better, but I wasn't sure I believed you then." A wide, bright smile spread over Helen's face. "I'm getting married!"

"Are you?" Violet asked. "Are you really? Tell me all about him."

"He's a barrister. I met him when I was handling some of Father's issues. We've been seeing each other since then. He knows about the baby, all of it, and he wants to marry me anyway."

Violet bit down on her bottom lip, both happy for Helen and yet still sad by her friend's past. She let Helen lead her into her rooms. It was a two-bedroom flat that the sisters shared when Anna wasn't in school. They had a private bath, a small kitchen, parlor, and dining room. The rooms were small, but they were nice.

Violet was seated in the tiny parlor and then Helen disappeared for tea and biscuits. When she returned, her face was glowing with happiness.

"What brings you by?" Helen asked.

"We've heard that your father isn't in prison. I was worried about you."

Helen's smile dimmed and she sighed. "I talked to Mr. Wakefield's friend, Detective Barnes, about that. He came by after Father got out. I already told Detective Barnes that Father wouldn't let me visit after the first time. I went to see him after the baby. When I came back to England," Helen swallowed and looked down at her hands. "We both wanted to apologize to each other. We did. And...and I haven't seen him since then. He stopped writing about a year later. I wrote to him every week. Something that I hoped would give him a bit of brightness, but he hasn't replied in at least a year."

Violet reached out to Helen and took her hand. "Did you know that Mr. Danvers was a blackmailer?"

Helen's mouth dropped open in surprise and she shook her head. "I—I—" Helen blinked rather rapidly, composing herself, and her gaze was fixed past Violet's shoulder. It was a long moment before she spoke. "I'm not surprised, actually. I was when you said it, but I'm not now." Helen met Violet's gaze and then she frowned. "Why?"

Violet had to order herself to be brave as she said, "My stepmother was his victim back then. Someone else has taken up the torch."

"You think it's my father?" Helen's voice was almost gentle. "It could be. Now that he's free. Or perhaps whoever helped him get out did so for that money."

Violet met Helen's gaze and the two of them looked at each other. "I didn't want to hurt you by asking."

"I accepted a long time ago that my father wasn't what I wanted him to be."

Violet squeezed Helen's hand tightly. "I didn't want to ruin our friendship, either. But—this secret concerns more than just my stepmother. The other party is innocent."

"I suppose it's Isolde," Helen guessed. She patted the back of Violet's hand. "You're a good sister. I think about you often when I try to be good for Anna. Don't feel bad for asking, but Violet—I have no idea who got my father out of prison and wherever he is—it isn't here."

Violet nodded and then asked Helen about her wedding plans. They spoke of pleasant things for a while before Violet asked, "Do you have any idea who else might have known about the Danvers's blackmailing scheme?"

Helen shook her head. "I was just the bit on the side. He didn't care about me. He didn't care about anyone."

"He got what was coming to him," Violet said without remorse. Carlton Danvers had been murdered by his own son. It might seem cold to say that he deserved it, but Violet didn't care. He had been a reprehensible man.

"He did," Helen agreed. "My father did too. They ruined people, destroyed their fortunes, and left them beggars. If not for you, my sister and I would be just as homeless and ruined. I'm not sorry to say that I don't feel a whole lot of remorse that they had to pay for their crimes."

"Even your father?"

Helen nodded. "They weren't stupid. All either of them had to do was turn their mind to good, and they could have been wealthy all the same. The hardest things in my life were directly associated to them. Vi, I gave my baby up. I did it because I loved her and knew she would have a better life than I could give her, but I gave her up. I can't forgive Danvers for that. And I won't forgive my father for bringing a monster into our lives and not warning me. Every day, I think about her. Every day, I love her, pray for her, and hate my father and Carlton a little harder that she couldn't be mine. I didn't help my father escape. I wouldn't have even if I had an idea about how to do it."

"Everyone thinks they'll get away with their crimes. They never seem to think about how the people they love will be affected. Not until it's too late."

Violet stayed long enough to ensure that Helen wasn't

overly upset and then promised to come to the small ceremony that Helen and her fiancé were planning. They didn't intend to wait, and Violet endorsed it.

Vi had taken a black cab to visit Helen, and rather than going home after the visit where she'd have to face her family and the case, she went to her favorite boutique. Alone, she flipped through dresses and looked at lingerie. She thought of Jack when she found the lacy nighties and she thought of Ginny when she found a beautiful pink kimono.

Ginny's favorite color was pink, and Violet wanted her ward to be utterly certain that she was adored without quibbling. Vi wandered through the shop and found herself buying Ginny a pink day dress and a nice gown for the theater. Given that Ginny was skipping out on school before the Christmas holidays, perhaps they should visit the theater. With Algie. And see if they could spot a blackmailer.

Was taking Ginny to a play, where a blackmailer might strike, bad form for a parental figure? Violet shrugged and then decided that Ginny had been through far too much to pretend otherwise.

Violet let her planning go as she examined a long evening gown with a deep vee at the chest all the way to the waist. It was a dark brown dress threaded with gold, and the slim gold chain at the waist was all that tucked the dress in and prevented it from showing everything there was to see to the world.

Violet tried it on to the shop-girl's delight and then bought it, plus gold evening shoes to match. Was it too racy? Perhaps. Was there an edge of revenge in it, knowing that Jack wouldn't love that Violet was showing quite so much of herself? Definitely. She didn't begrudge him using his skills to make the world a better place, but she knew that this blackmail investigation without him made her feel lonelier than their cold bed.

When Violet left the dress shop, a man stepped up next to her. She started until she realized it was the pretty Mr. Smith.

"If Mathers was on the street," he told her, "he could have snatched you as easily as Danvers took your sister."

"But Mathers isn't on the street, it's you." Violet turned to face him and asked, "Why are you trying to scare me?"

"Whoever is blackmailing your stepmother could be as big of a monster as Hugo Danvers once was."

"So could that fellow or that fellow," Violet said, nodding to the next two passing men. "I don't want to live in a cage because of what could be."

"It would hurt Beatrice if anything happened to you. You're the star in her skies, Mrs. Jack."

"Mrs. Jack?"

He didn't explain himself, but there was enough of a glint in his eyes to challenge her. Violet, however, didn't mind Jack's name. Whether Wakefield or Jack, she was his as he was hers.

"Did you get into the prison?"

"In, out, through."

"Through?" Violet shot back.

"I'd feel better taking you home, ma'am."

Violet let him hail another black cab and seat her in it. He followed and then sat across from her.

"Why are you worried?"

"Someone killed Mathers."

Violet stared at the man.

"Someone killed him and hid his body in the prison. He never escaped. He was executed by someone who was careful enough to get away with it."

Violet leaned slowly back. "What happened?"

"From what I can tell?" Smith's frown deepened. "A guard called Mathers from his cell. Mathers never came back. The guard disappeared as well. At first, it was assumed by the warden that the guard helped get Mathers out and then fled himself. But none of the regular guards were unaccounted for then or now."

Violet shivered. "What a terrible way to die. Helen Mathers said she hadn't visited her father in some time."

"She hadn't," Smith agreed. "But someone did. Quite often. Their name on the visitor's log was obscured. No one remembers just what they looked like. I would guess that the guards were paid to look the other way and Mathers's disappearance has given them good reasons to remain forgetful."

"Dead?" Violet asked with a shiver. "Are you certain? You saw the body?"

"Murdered," Smith told Violet flatly. "The fellow who took Mathers out isn't the type of man who lets a prisoner go. I found where the body was disposed of, and I have no doubt that Mathers was murdered. Horribly I think. I don't know what your stepmother stepped in, Mrs. Jack, but it stinks. "

Violet wasn't comforted at the sight of her home, her brother Gerald walking slowly up the steps, or the knowledge that Jack hadn't backed off on the guards on their home after the last round of incidents. Was there an extra man or two about? Yes. Were they armed? Yes.

Would she still be sleeping with her derringer in the drawer next to her bed? Yes. Very much so.

Violet let Smith walk her up the steps and didn't object when he disappeared into the house towards Beatrice's office. It didn't surprise Violet that he knew just where to go, and it wouldn't surprise her later if she found him going through her things.

Before he got far, however, Violet said, "I have some letters for you to read, Mr. Smith. We'll be looking into who might have known the particulars of them and who would use that information against my family."

CHAPTER 13

From the tone of his letter, Jack was worried, and he didn't even know about the body yet. When he found out Harry Mathers was dead? She suspected he would react in either a furious tirade or his presence at the door.

Violet faced the chalkboard. She'd expected to find Gerald and Victor in the parlor when she entered, but they weren't there. She hoped that somehow Victor was able to comfort Gerald. Violet had written Lottie Wilder two notes herself, but the girl had yet to reply. Either she wasn't getting Violet's notes or Lottie had determined to break ties.

"Violet!" Gerald called from the doorway to the parlor. "Quick! We need a dinner."

Vi turned in confusion.

"Lottie is coming. She told her parents that she's going to the pictures with a friend, but the friend is going to bring her here."

"She's coming?" Violet repeated, hardly daring to hope.

Gerald nodded. His skin was white with ruddy circles. He looked as if he might break down right in front of her.

Vi didn't hesitate. She glanced at the clock and then rang the bell for Hargreaves, their plans to eat out immediately aborted in favor of dining in. Cook would be frustrated, but Violet wasn't above bribes or begging, which she did the moment Hargreaves appeared.

"I—I did what you said," Gerald told her shakily once the dinner plans were in motion. "I wrote to her. I bribed a boy to put it into her hands at the park. I begged, Vi. I promised her the house on the other side of the park from you. I begged, I painted, I did it all."

Violet crossed to him, tugged him to one of the armchairs, and shoved him down. A moment later, she handed him a whiskey. He sipped at it like it was water after a day in the desert.

"Slow down," Vi advised. "I'm not going to let her see you in your cups."

Gerald stared at Violet and then muttered, "I have been entirely unmanned."

Her wicked laugh agreed, and he shot her a disgusted look, but it was followed by grabbing her hand to squeeze it. "I wouldn't have gotten this far without you, Vi."

Victor appeared a moment later and took in the scene. "Touching. Stiff upper lip, darlings. Eleanor has arrived."

"Uh-oh." Violet darted across the room to the box of letters.

She gathered it up and then turned frantically looking for a place to hide it. Victor nodded towards the window where a small chair stood. Violet put the box on the chair and then Victor put a cushion on top.

"What's all this?" Gerald demanded.

The twins ignored him to stare at the ridiculous box. Violet grabbed the curtain, yanking the cord that tied it back, and freed it. She pulled the curtain around the chair and then stared at the most obvious hiding place that had ever been created.

"Sit, look innocent," Victor told her.

Violet darted across the floor and spun the chalk-board around. It was double-sided, and the second side was perfectly clean. Vi dove for a chair next to Gerald as Hargreaves opened a door. Vi was gasping as she stole Gerald's drink and used it to hide her shaking breath.

Lady Eleanor stepped into the room, looking at the three utterly silent siblings. "What's all this?" Her cool voice was tinged with suspicion. "Conspiring?"

"We leave that to you, madam," Gerald told her.

"Mother or Lady Eleanor, please."

Gerald's gaze narrowed on their stepmother, and she flushed lightly. "Careful."

"Or what?"

"Father won't live forever," Gerald said with overt threat. "Then it will just be you and me."

Lady Eleanor's gaze widened in horror. Victor handed her a cocktail. He'd made them to cover for the reason he had been standing, and to gather himself. He crossed to Violet and Gerald with a tray that held three more. Violet took one, as did Gerald.

"A drink in each hand, Violet?" Lady Eleanor's gaze

turned to the blank chalkboard and then she muttered, "I should have known that you'd be useless. Nothing on your board, no progress. Have you done anything?"

Violet sipped her drink as she set aside Gerald's whiskey. She considered how to answer now that her racing breath was under control. Her gaze moved to Victor who was eyeing her back. Both of them wanted to lash out, but they also didn't want to cause a family war. When you came down to the end of things, Isolde and Geoffrey loved their mother.

Violet sipped her drink again and promised, "Progress is being made."

"Why should I believe you? Have you even found Mathers?"

"I'm aware of where he is."

"What now?" Victor exclaimed in surprise and Gerald stared at Violet, who shook her head very slightly.

"He needs to be back in prison. Call on your husband and that friend of his, have Mathers yanked back to jail and put in the farthest corner."

"Ham and Jack are in Leeds, Lady Eleanor," Violet said. "The Mathers situation is being handled."

"Well, get them here," she hissed. "What's the point of having the family sullied with Scotland Yard if we aren't benefited?"

"No," Violet said evenly. "I won't call the two people in my family you've tried most to alienate because it's convenient for you."

"You owe me," Lady Eleanor snapped.

"No," Gerald declared, "she doesn't."

"You don't get to decide that, Gerald. Need I remind you that you aren't the earl?" Lady Eleanor's cold gaze met Gerald's hard glint, and then she was glancing away. It was a retreat, but she tried to play it off as scorn.

Gerald, however, lifted a brow, his gaze cold and hate-filled. "You can count on Violet, Eleanor. Now leave."

"Excuse me?" She dared a quick glance.

"Leave," he told her. "Leave now. Violet will look after you, not that you deserve it."

"I am the matron of this family," Lady Eleanor reminded him with a scowl. "You can't just order me away."

"Violet has held the role of matron since the moment she stepped in and took care of Isolde when you didn't."

Violet stood and took Lady Eleanor by the hand. She didn't want to deal with more family squabbling. Not when there was a dinner to plan and Gerald's engagement to save. "I promise I am working on your problem. I promise I will do all that can be done to find out who is harassing you. And—I promise you—this will come to an end."

"Mathers will go back to prison?"

"He won't be a problem anymore," Violet swore. "He's already in hand."

Lady Eleanor left, protesting, but Gerald's scorn-filled gaze chased her out far better than anything Violet or Victor could do or say. The moment the door was shut both brothers turned on Violet.

"Smith founds Mathers?" Victor demanded. "How?"

"According to him, he broke into, through, and out of the prison. Along the way, he realized what happened to Mathers and his location."

"But not who helped him?"

"Murdered him," Violet corrected. "Harry Mathers was murdered. He never left prison. He was killed and disposed of in a way that made it seem he escaped."

Victor's mouth dropped open. "Bloody hell."

"You need to call Jack," Gerald ordered Victor.

"I'm going to tell Jack," Violet protested. "You don't need to do anything."

Gerald ignored Violet and repeated, "Telephone. No delays. The moment you find out something like that, any delay is unforgivable."

Victor glanced at Violet, giving her an apologetic look. "He's right, Vi."

"I'm not going to lie to Jack. I'll tell him. I don't need either of you to interfere."

"It isn't about you, Vi," Gerald told her flatly. "A man needs to know his woman is safe."

"Excuse me?" Violet asked with silky threat.

Gerald was entirely unbothered despite the praise of moments before. He met her angry gaze and shrugged without remorse. "That friendship you appreciate between Victor and Jack gets killed in moments like these. There's only one course of action that Jack would accept."

Violet leaned back and shook her head. "You're all idiots."

"Be that as it may be," Victor said. "I agree with Gerald. If Kate were dabbling in a murder and Jack didn't tell me, we'd have more than words. It would be fisticuffs and decades of anger."

Violet rolled her eyes and leaned back, sipping the last of her cocktail. "Give him my regards."

"It's not Jack's fault that Gerald and I agree," Victor

said, taking the cocktail glass from her hand and pulling her to her feet.

Violet let Victor tug her to the library where their telephone was housed. It took long minutes to get Jack on the other end, and despite the distance and the crackling on the line, she could make out his string of curses as Victor explained the situation. A moment later, Victor handed Violet the receiver and then left her to it.

"Violet?"

"Jack?"

He paused. "You're angry."

Violet had to think before she answered, but there was a delay between them, so it gave her a moment. "I'm all right."

"Mathers was murdered in prison?"

"So Smith says."

"Is there any reason to believe you aren't all right, Vi?"

She found herself staring in shock at the shelves in front of her. He wasn't leaping on the next train to come in, sword and shield ready? She couldn't be certain if she should feel more pleased that he was trusting in her abilities or disappointed that she wouldn't see him quite sooner. "We don't know anything, Jack. Nothing beyond what I already wrote to you. Our best suspects are the same ones we considered when Danvers died. Eleanor lies. Everyone is hedging. If I were worried about people digging into what I was up to, I wouldn't be afraid of anything Victor and I know because it is next to nothing."

Jack paused and then said, "Don't go out alone."

"Are you all right?"

"Yes. We've got him, I think. But I can't go yet, Vi. Not if you're all right."

"I'm fine," she promised him softly.

"You swear it?"

Violet nodded and then realized what she was doing and said, "I swear it. I won't go out alone. I won't do anything stupid."

"Carry your gun, be safe, use all those wits you have."

Violet found that her eyes were burning with tears. Nearly every day they woke wrapped around each other, every night she fell asleep to the melody of his heartbeat and the comfort of his breathing. "You be safe."

"I will," he said.

"Swear it."

"I swear it."

She paused and found that the burning had turned to tears and one had dripped onto her hand. "I love you, Jack Wakefield. Carry your gun, don't do stupid things without Ham, and remember that you've stolen all of me, Jack. If something happens to you, I won't be all right."

"Then we'll both be safe, armed, and careful," he said. "Because you've stolen all of me as well, darling."

Violet hung up before the few tears turned to sobs and they made some eavesdropping operator blush. She ran up the stairs to her bedroom, eyed their lonely bed, and found her way to her beloved bath. She was going with hot enough to cook herself, lavender oils to calm herself, and the sheer hope that if she held her breath long enough, somehow Jack being gone would be all right.

Violet soaked a long time and then considered her new scandalous dress before she selected a black gown for dinner instead. Her dress was beaded and had a train that just hovered above the floor when she wore her tallest heels. Violet wrapped her throat with her turquoise beads and brushed her hair before she added a flowered headband made of pearls and diamonds. Rather than loading on the bangles and more diamonds, Violet added her spider ring, renewed her cosmetics, and left her bedroom.

When she reached the area outside of the dining room, Lottie hadn't arrived. For once it was someone else pacing. Gerald had dressed in an evening suit as well. It was his, so he must have come prepared. His face was freshly shaved, his hair slicked back, he was pale, but the frantic pacing had added color.

"He wants another whiskey," Victor told her. "But I refused."

"He can't properly get on his knees if he can barely stand," Violet agreed. "I don't know what to do."

"Think of how I feel then, Vi darling. We all know I have half the wits you do. I want to throw myself at her feet, and beg her to put him out of his misery."

CHAPTER 14

*C*harlotte Wilder had dressed for the occasion, but she had put a long coat over the top to hide her soft pink evening gown. Her neck and ears were bare of jewels, but her long silky curls hung about her ivory neck as beautiful as any diamond necklace. Her eyes were wide and shining and when they landed on Gerald, they warmed.

The two of them stared at each other with a tension that crackled. Violet bit down on her bottom lip to stop herself from begging them to choose each other.

"I'm sorry," Lottie said quietly.

Gerald folded in on himself, turning stark white.

"No!" Lottie said, scrambling. She darted to him, throwing herself at him. "I'm sorry I had to think. I'm sorry I didn't throw myself right at you. I'm sorry I let the countess get inside my mind. I'm sorry."

Gerald staggered back as she landed in his arms, but he grasped her tightly.

"I'm sorry," he echoed. "I'm sorry she's my stepmother and I can't get rid of her. I'm sorry that your father doesn't like me. I'm sorry that you had to choose anything."

Violet watched and found that Victor was pressing his handkerchief in her hands. She dabbed away the unnoticed tears as the two lovers whispered.

Violet glanced at Victor who grinned back.

"Should we leave?" he mouthed to her.

Violet glanced at the couple. Gerald was pressing a kiss to Lottie's palm. His gaze was so fixed on hers, he didn't seem to notice their audience.

Violet answered her twin with a shrug. Should they leave? Should they stay? Violet took a slow step backwards towards the door and her movement caught Gerald's attention. He laughed as Lottie turned in time to see them backing away.

"Don't go," Lottie said happily. "I—" Lottie glanced up at Gerald and then at Violet. "Thank you, Violet. I wouldn't have been able to trust it without you. If you hadn't been so kind—"

Violet smiled away the gratitude and gestured the couple into the dining room. They ate in a blur of watching Gerald and Lottie making happy plans while the other two missed their spouses even more.

"Is it wrong," Victor asked Violet while they left the dining room, "to go and get my wife and take her away from her ailing mother?"

"Yes," Violet told him, simply.

Victor scowled and then glanced with envy at Gerald, who was tucking Lottie into his side in the parlor. They hadn't been wise enough to have the chalkboard moved away and Lottie stared at it before she left Gerald on the sofa to turn it around and read it.

"Who are these people?" Lottie asked, staring at the list of names that Violet had put down the last time she and Victor worked on it. Violet was glad Lottie's name was no longer on the list.

"Those were our suspects when Carlton Danvers died," Victor explained.

"Henry Carlyle?"

The twins looked at each other and then shrugged in silent unison.

"That's your father the earl, isn't it?"

Violet sniffed and then admitted, "If Father knew the details of who and what Carlton Danvers was—"

"Any loving father would have slaughtered the man like a rabid dog," Gerald told Lottie. "The only reason that Father wasn't a good suspect was that he'd have done it before the wedding day."

"The wedding day?" Lottie asked.

"Our little sister was getting ready to flee," Violet said. "I had gone for Father to tell him she wasn't going to go through with the wedding. But instead, I found Danvers." Violet shivered and added, "It was horrible."

Lottie gasped. "You found his body?"

Violet remembered the body in the library, the spread of blood, the smell. She gagged, and then let Victor pull her close as she nodded.

Lottie looked back at the chalkboard. "And you thought your father might have done it?"

"Not really," Violet said. "But you can't set aside

family as a suspect if anyone else would suspect them. The most likely person to murder you," Violet told Lottie, "is your father or Gerald."

She gasped. Her eyes were wide. Her pretty lips were gaping. She glanced between the three siblings, probably looking for one of them to be joking, but no one was laughing.

"For me?" Violet continued. "Father, Gerald, Victor, and Jack of course."

"Of course?" Lottie gasped.

Violet nodded as Gerald cursed. "Change the subject, Violet. Neither myself nor Mr. Wilder are going to lay a hand on Lottie, and Jack would commit a hundred murders before he let anyone hurt you."

Violet fiddled with her wedding ring and tried smiling at Lottie. "It's just the likelihood, Lottie. Most men don't hurt the women they love. My brother never would."

Lottie shivered and let Gerald pull her to the seat. They had wine with dinner, but when Victor offered to make cocktails, Violet requested her favorite ginger wine and found that Lottie had joined her. They discussed wedding plans again.

"Oddly enough," Violet said with a smile, "this is the second round of wedding plans I've discussed today. Helen Mathers is getting married. They aren't going to wait."

"Neither are we," Gerald said. "You can have the biggest wedding you want, Lottie, that can be done in the shortest amount of time."

VIOLET PACED her bedroom that night as she thought about Jack. What was happening in Leeds if he wasn't coming back with a murder in London? There were prayers fervent enough for the worry she was carrying. She wanted to kick the wall, to shriek at the heavens, but she couldn't.

Her door cracked and she met Victor's equally sleepless gaze. He'd taken to remaining at her house since his was too empty. "Jack isn't coming back?"

Violet's lip was trembling as she shook her head. Victor opened his arms, and she was in them before she even realized she was crossing the room. "What will I do if—"

"Don't," Victor ordered. "Don't."

"But what if?"

"It's not going to happen," Victor said, but she heard the same worry in his voice. She pressed her face into her brother's chest and wished that the sound of his heartbeat provided the same comfort of Jack's.

"I want to get on a train and go," she admitted.

"You can't."

Violet didn't need Victor to tell her that. If something bad was happening in Leeds—and it was—Jack would be at greater risk if Violet were there. She was his Achilles heel.

"I might vomit," she told him.

Victor squeezed her tightly and then shoved her to her bed. He put her small writing desk on her lap and handed her paper and a pen. Without letting her mind linger on Jack, Victor pushed Violet through story ideas and plots until she found her eyes were drooping.

Victor picked up the book they were writing a sequel for and read to Violet until she slipped into sleep.

She didn't wake until the next morning and had to wonder what tender mercies of heaven made that possible. Violet dressed in a cherry red day dress and went down to the parlor. To her surprise, Victor was standing at the bar with a good dozen cocktail concoctions in front of him. On the other side of the bar were Smith and Beatrice.

"Oh," Violet said. "It's not even 9:00 a.m."

"I'm creating. Beatrice won't do more than sip, and even then only if I ask for feedback. Smith apparently doesn't have a limit."

"It's the devil in him," Violet said. She crossed to them. "Which one is the best?"

Beatrice tapped the fourth glass of the dozen. Violet lifted it, sipped it, and then nodded. "That's lovely. Insomnia?"

Victor clarified, "Vi's insomnia. Bitter, biting, and somehow still sweet."

Violet met his gaze and novels of feeling passed between them before they turned to Smith. He had changed, shaved, and was bright-eyed. "Did you find the letters?"

"Beatrice got them for me. Your stepmother is a nightmare."

Violet sighed and, keeping the half-empty fourth glass, crossed to an overstuffed chair. "She's a typical well-bred Englishwoman who was raised to prize being an aristocrat above all else. She made the same choice as generations of idiots."

Beatrice cleared her throat before she said, "It seems to me that Mr. Mitchell Fitzhugh truly loved Lady Eleanor. I don't know that I find him that suspicious."

"The biggest victim if this secret gets out will be Geoffrey," Violet said. "Or it could be if Father doesn't mock the rumor and claim Geoffrey."

"Which he would," Victor said. "However, Fitzhugh couldn't know that."

"Exactly my point," Smith declared. "Love twists to hate. Maybe he decided he hates the countess and it was time for revenge."

"I don't believe it," Beatrice told Smith in a way that suggested they'd argued about it before this. "I think he truly loves her. Or loved her when he wrote those letters."

"Regardless of the answer," Violet cut in, making Beatrice blush, "we need to speak with Fitzhugh. I want to see the look in his eyes when we ask him if he's threatening Geoffrey with awareness of who he is."

"Father's back in London with Geoffrey," Victor said. "Ginny stayed. She had an important exam."

Vi grinned and her relief was echoed by Victor's. "Speaking of Ginny," Violet told Beatrice. "Would you have one of the housemaids pack up the things I bought Ginny and see them delivered?"

Beatrice nodded, making a note in her notebook.

"She's not your maid anymore," Smith told Violet.

Vi paused but Beatrice snapped, "I am happy to do as Violet asks."

"That's the statement of a maid pretending to be a business woman."

Beatrice's gaze narrowed and the look she sent Smith actually had him wince.

Violet considered and then said, "I'll take care of it, Beatrice."

"No!" Beatrice argued. "I work for you."

"He's right, though," Violet said. "My apologies."

If the look Smith received before had been scathing, the one Beatrice gave him after Violet's apology was deathly. Violet begged Victor for help with a glance.

"I agree with Beatrice," Victor said offhandedly and turned back to the cocktails. "I read the letters this morning. I also think we should consider something else."

Violet turned to him. She kept her gaze focused on him so she didn't have to see the silent battle between Beatrice and Smith.

"I would have known your secret, Vi. I made my own list of suspects."

Victor gestured to the chalkboard and Violet realized it had been pulled out, so he could see it while he played at the bar.

Violet stood and turned the chalkboard to read it. It said:

PEOPLE WHO MIGHT HAVE KNOWN E'S SECRET

Helen Mathers

Harry Mathers

Markus Kennington

Wanda Kennington

Norman Kennington

Adele Kennington

Carlton Danvers

Henry Carlyle

Mitchell Fitzhugh

Violet looked at the list that Victor had created and her head tilted as she examined it. "You made the list longer."

"I'm not looking for the blackmailer," Victor said. "I was just thinking about us. Who might know or have learned Lady Eleanor's secret? Wouldn't it have to be someone close to her or close to someone she would confide in?"

Violet nibbled her thumb as she considered.

"Then there are Algie's secrets," Violet mused. "Which aren't that hard to find really, but still, they aren't written on his forehead. It is possible someone associated with him or with Lady Eleanor could have gotten the information on them both."

She took the chalk and crossed out names until it read:

Helen Mathers

Harry Mathers

Markus Kennington

Wanda Kennington

Norman Kennington

Adele Kennington

Carlton Danvers

Henry Carlyle

Mitchell Fitzhugh

Victor stood next to Violet. "If you add in someone who might have the connections or wherewithal to have a man murdered in prison—"

He crossed out more names until only three remained.

Markus Kennington

Norman Kennington

Henry Carlyle

Violet reached out and crossed out their father's name. Only two names were left and they were both Eleanor's brothers. The twins looked at each other and then back at the chalkboard.

"That assumes," Smith said, "that someone else didn't know about Danvers's blackmailing, contacted Mathers, and promised something—anything—to get Danvers's stash of proof. That person could be anyone."

"You can, however, start with the Kennington men," Beatrice told him. "While Violet and her family work on Lady Eleanor about who else might have known her secrets."

"The best plan," Violet said, "is for my father to tell Eleanor that he will claim Geoffrey no matter what. That will take the sting from the blackmail threat. Then we see what happens."

"Set your man of business on them as well," Victor suggested. "As memory serves, both of the Kennington brothers were involved in Danvers's fraudulent invest-ment scheme. Maybe one of them is more hard-pressed than the other."

"I need to see Helen again," Violet said with a sigh. "Does anyone know what you know, Smith?"

Smith shook his head.

"We can't let her find out about her father when it all comes tumbling out. She deserves the warning."

Smith stood and announced, "I'll start with the Kennington brothers and Fitzhugh. You can't rule him out yet." Smith nodded at both Violet and Victor, glanced at Beatrice and said, "I'll be seeing you."

Her scowl made him smirk and then he was gone.

Violet considered. "He's right, you realize," she said to her twin. "We can't rule out Fitzhugh. But we can try."

Victor caught her meaning at once and agreed with a nod.

CHAPTER 15

*V*iolet and Victor were both pacing the next afternoon as they waited for the knock at the door. The silence was tense enough that it stifled the whole room. They bypassed each other as they moved. The teacart was loaded with sandwiches, coffee, and an excellent blend of black tea. The room was shining, the chalkboard missing, all signs of the bar being a playground hidden.

Victor wore a conservative grey suit, a blue tie, and a tense jaw. Violet wore a light tan day dress that hung to her calves. Her powder was light, her lipstick just enough to add a little color, and her stomach was roiling.

The knock had both of the twins leaping and Violet let out a sick laugh. They crossed to the armchairs near the lit fireplace and sat side-by-side as they faced the door.

The man who followed Hargreaves in had them

gaping. White blonde hair, watery blue eyes, a stick-thin frame without an ounce of fat.

"Oh my heavens," Violet murmured, unable to hold her thoughts back. "I—"

The man smiled at them and glanced around the room. "Yes, I thought so."

"I—" Violet repeated and then looked at Victor. No doubt her own expression matched the shell-shocked astonishment of her twin.

"Yes, I look just like him."

Violet was suddenly uncertain that Father claiming Geoffrey would be sufficient to save her brother from being the cuckoo in the nest.

"Bloody hell, Fitzhugh," Victor groaned. "It's like looking into the future."

"No wonder Geoffrey knows you look in on him."

Fitzhugh took the chair that Violet was slow to offer and she poured him tea in a shocked haze. She loaded him a plate with blindness, her mind racing around the thoughts of her brother.

"I wanted him to know I care," Fitzhugh said. "I didn't want him to think I didn't."

Violet pressed her fingers against her lips, ignoring the coffee and food, and tried to think. "I feel like all my questions have shifted."

Mr. Fitzhugh smiled at her rather gently. "Perhaps you could start with why you pretended my son wanted to meet me."

Violet leaned back and then decided nothing ventured, nothing gained. "We were curious if you were the person blackmailing Lady Eleanor about Geoffrey's parentage."

Mr. Fitzhugh's gaze narrowed and a look of shocking fury crossed his face. In a low, angry voice, he said, "I would never. Why would you think such a thing?"

"Because," Victor said, "you clearly know the secret."

"Anyone who knew us then could guess," Mr. Fitzhugh said. "Every Kennington, your Father, perhaps some of Ellie's oldest friends. It's not a hard leap if you know me and have seen him."

"Yes, obviously," Violet said. She was flabbergasted.

"I won't pretend to love Ellie anymore," Mr. Fitzhugh added, "but I do love my son."

Violet's man of business would confirm that there was no reason for Fitzhugh to set aside his personal honor to blackmail the mother of his child, but Violet liked the man. She hadn't intended to. Someone who had truly loved Lady Eleanor started out with very low expectations on Violet's part, but somehow the earnest fierceness and care that Fitzhugh directed only towards Geoffrey was all that Violet needed.

"Do you have any idea who might blackmail her?" Victor asked, not quibbling with Fitzhugh's claims.

Fitzhugh shook his head. He was upset when he asked, "What are your father's intentions? Does he know?"

"He's always known," Violet told him. "Father will do what can be done to protect Geoffrey."

"It would help," Fitzhugh murmured, "if he didn't look so much like me."

"Or if you weren't around," Victor said.

The two men gazed at each other. It was the sort of things dogs did before they decided who was in charge.

Violet shook her head and sipped her coffee, waiting for the posturing to end.

"I've always intended to spend some time in the Virgin Islands," Mr. Fitzhugh said, resigned. "I could use a holiday."

Violet bit down on her bottom lip as the man sighed. His gaze was direct when he looked at Violet.

"There isn't anything else I can do for him, is there?"

Violet shook her head. She had to admit that she believed the worried agony in his voice. "You can trust us to look after him."

"You're Lady Penelope's children, aren't you?"

"We are," Victor agreed.

"He's not even your brother."

"Of course he is," Violet snapped. "You might have fathered him, but he's ours."

Mr. Fitzhugh looked between the twins and he sighed again. "This is why you tend your own garden."

Violet shifted.

"Sowing someone else's bed leaves you powerless. I lost my son before he was born, but I've never been comfortable with that fact. Tell him I care."

"We will," Victor agreed.

"Tell him that he can reach out to me whenever he might need to. I fear I've never stopped failing him, but I'd like to make amends if he wants me to."

"He's young yet," Violet told Mr. Fitzhugh. "Give him time."

Violet watched him go. "I fear that we're no further ahead," she said to Victor.

"We are significantly further ahead," Victor said, "in the parts that matter. We will be able to tell Geoffrey we met his first father, confirm that Geoffrey has always been loved by the man, and that we respect him. That will matter to our little brother."

Violet nodded and then said, "Dinner and the theater with Algie. Hopefully another piece of the puzzle."

"I'm tired of this puzzle," Victor muttered. "I want to go back to the country, with my wife and daughters, and throw my energy into a cocktail recipe book and Carlyle Fine Wines & Spirits. How do we end up involved in these messes, Vi?"

Violet wished she had an answer.

⁓

VIOLET DRESSED CAREFULLY. A red and gold dress, embroidered with dragons. It was floor-length and luxurious. She layered on the jewelry and her mink coat and found her brother in the hall as polished and shiny as she was.

"Wish us clues and criminals, Hargreaves," Victor said cheerily. To Violet he added, "Gerald received our invitation. He and Lottie are coming, eyes at the ready, et cetera, et cetera."

Violet followed Victor down the stairs, was handed into the back of the auto, and they arrived at Hotel Saffron to meet their cousin and brother. Algie was half-zozzled before dinner and by the end, he was fully in his cups. He giggled the entirety of the journey between the hotel and the theater until Gerald murmured to Lottie, "I'll never do that to you, love."

Clara laughed and declared, "Never believe it. They're all promises in the beginning, but the next thing you know, they're having their pants let out and sleeping through the theater."

The usher led them up to the box that had been reserved. It was directly across from the one that Lady Eleanor usually used. With Lady Eleanor were Geoffrey, both of her brothers, her sisters-in-law, and a young woman that had Lottie paling.

"What is the matter?" Violet asked.

"That's Genevieve Bromley."

"She doesn't matter," Gerald told his betrothed. "I swear. She's nothing to me."

"She might be lovely," Violet suggested and Gerald groaned her name while Lottie gaped, "but she's missing the most important accessory."

"What is that?" Lottie asked, still too pale.

Algie's wife, Clara, answered with a merry laugh, "That massive rock on your finger, kitten. That's the gold medal, the blue ribbon, the chain. Nothing else matters."

"Mmm," Violet agreed, twisting her own wedding ring. "Nothing says you're taken and beloved like a stone and an announcement in the paper."

"It's tomorrow morning," Gerald said. "I swear. I talked to Lottie's father, did not receive his blessing, and said I was going to marry her, love her, and earn that blessing eventually."

"How'd they take that?" Victor asked as the orchestra tuned.

"They're resigned, I think," Lottie said. "Mother says I've always been stubborn. Father makes dark predictions. My little sisters whisper it's romantic."

They took their seats, accepted the champagne flutes that were delivered to the box, and Violet watched her stepmother's box while the play started. Their gazes were fixated anywhere but on their box save for Geoffrey, who lifted a hand, smirked when Lady Eleanor scolded him, and then boldly winked at Violet and Lottie.

"It's dire," Victor whispered, "that her siblings are with her as they're our current best suspects."

"I wonder if they know we're helping her," Vi murmured back.

"It wouldn't surprise me," Victor said, "if she didn't tell them a thing."

Violet snorted when Algie let out a loud snore which was followed by Clara's laughter. Lottie glanced at Violet, grinned at the spectacle, and then she leaned across Victor to say to Violet, "Promise me you won't let me become snobbish."

"Promised," Violet announced.

"Impossible," Gerald whispered.

The box next to them shushed them, but Algie snorted again, and the laughter broke through the tense moment on the stage. By the time the play ended, nothing worth noting had happened. The crowd to leave the theater was thick and they were unable to do anything other than slide towards the exit and their ways home. As they reached the sidewalk, Algie glanced at the others, reached into his pocket, and pulled out another note.

"Didn't feel a thing," Algie giggled. "By Jove!"

"What are they blackmailing you about, Algie?"

His ears were dark red as he glanced at his wife. "I'm afraid I had a relationship with a—ah—lady of the night. There was a result."

Clara frowned.

"I wanted to take her, raise her, but her mother found quite a rich protector and threw me away. I was heartbroken, I say. Heartbroken."

Violet gaped at her cousin who was blushing deeply.

"What happened to the child?"

"She's in a French nunnery. Being raised like a lady. I pay for it. Her mother died not too long after she threw me away. I asked Aunt Agatha what to do, and she suggested the location. They're good ladies there. Fresh air, all that."

"How old is she?" Violet asked.

Algie swallowed and then muttered, "Five. She's five years old. Clara said we're going to get her, raise her, and love her. It's the right thing to do now that we're married."

"I say," Gerald said, "I—"

"It is the right thing to do," Violet interrupted, shooting Gerald a dark look. "I look forward to meeting her."

"She's named Agatha too," Algie said. "Aunt Agatha—" Algie shook his head and admitted, "I thought she was going to murder me before I told her. But you know what? She wasn't cruel at all. She told me that the only thing that mattered was the baby and doing right by her."

Violet's fingers dug into Victor's wrist as she fought sudden tears at the loss of the woman.

"By heaven," Algie swore, "I miss her."

CHAPTER 16

"*A*re you surprised?" Violet asked Victor as they waited for their auto to pull up for them.

"No, not really."

Violet shot him a disbelieving look and he grinned at her, running his hand over his hair. "I wish Kate were here. I don't think I reacted well, and she would have. How do you say, 'Bloody hell, well, we'll love her regardless?'"

"Maybe just like that," Vi suggested.

"I'm surprised that he kept it a secret. I'm not surprised that he fell in love with his mistress. The fact that he probably offered to marry her and claim the baby and she turned him down is shocking."

Gerald scoffed and tucked Lottie closer. "Don't tell your father about Algie."

Violet choked on a laugh while Lottie patted Gerald's arm. "I'm not a complete ninny."

"You aren't a ninny at all," Gerald swore, pressing a kiss on her head. "Are we going home now?"

"My parents would prefer if I did," Lottie muttered, "but I'd rather have a longer break."

"I have been creating quite a delicious drink called Vi's Insomnia," Victor told them. "Come back to Vi's house with us and help me drain Jack's cellar before he returns."

"Sold," Gerald announced. He paused a moment and then frowned, "Geoffrey, lad?"

"I don't want to go home." He'd appeared from behind Violet, and she gasped as she turned.

"Come try my new cocktail," Victor invited.

Violet winced. "I have no desire to be the responsible one among us—"

"Then don't be." Victor's grand proclamation wasn't enough to stop Violet from elbowing him hard.

"—however, Lady Eleanor might murder us if we return Geoffrey to her half-zozzled. Even Father would frown on it."

"Only one cocktail for you lad," Victor said, slapping Geoffrey on the back.

Violet shook her head at both brothers, but she guessed that she'd never win this fight. Instead, she shot them a dark look. "Speaking of warts—"

"Hey," Geoffrey protested. "I was being good."

"I'm referring to Victor. If we insult you to your face, Geoffrey darling, it means we like you."

Their auto was only a few lengths from them when Geoffrey said, "Mother said you were a duo of betraying fiends to Genevieve Bromley and made up some hefty lie about Gerald's companion being your friend."

"Oh I say," Gerald said, "Lottie darling, meet our youngest brother, Geoffrey Carlyle—too often referred to as the wart. Lottie Wilder, soon to be Carlyle," Gerald said to Geoffrey. "Hoping you'd be my best man, old boy."

Geoffrey's eyes widened and Violet felt her own do the same. Hers burned with tears for both of her brothers. Geoffrey's cheeks had turned to a brilliant flush and he nodded, stammering an assent. Gerald shook hands manfully with Geoffrey, slapping him on the back. Given the amount of emotion between the two of them, the awkwardness of the handshake and the way they were not quite meeting each other's eyes, Violet had to shake her head. Men!

She glanced at Victor who was as pleased as she was, only he was far better at hiding his feelings, but they both knew what they'd just seen. In fact all of them knew it. It had been a claiming of Geoffrey. Blood related or not—they were family.

"All right," Violet told Geoffrey, "you can have a cocktail without objections."

He laughed and then muttered low, "Mother got a note like the one I saw Algie open. We were still on the stairs when he opened the note. I saw the whole thing. You were all so focused on it."

"Did all of you see the note?" Violet asked him as the auto finally stopped in front of them.

Geoffrey frowned. "You mean like my mother?"

"Your mother, your uncles and aunts."

Geoffrey shook his head. "Both Uncle Markus and Uncle Norman left the play early. Uncle Norman said something about not being able to handle another minute of the melodrama."

"What was your mother's reaction to her note?"

"She didn't read it. Just found it and tucked it into her handbag."

Violet hid her own reaction and let Victor seat her in the auto. She wished it were Jack handing her into the auto. She loved those dark journeys between one location and another when they would twine their fingers together and she leaned against his chest. There was something about the patter of the rain on the auto glass, the way the water splashed outside, but they were warm inside that made it seem as though they were cocooned together.

Vi tucked her mink coat closer, shivering in the darkness. She listened as the others chatted and couldn't help but realize how lucky they were that they'd become friends as they had over the last few years. For the longest time, Violet and Victor had been separated from the family, but it no longer mattered when they were together like this.

Violet laid her head on Victor's shoulder as they drove back to her house. The lights were on outside, and Violet caught the flash of one of their guards in the darkness between her house and the one next. The fellow watched as they made their way up the steps.

Violet watched the fellow fade back into the shadows while Hargreaves opened the door for them. As they reached the parlor, they found their return had been expected by their father. Hargreaves took coats while Father was introduced to Lottie.

Her eyes were wide, and her hands were shaking, but

she smiled charmingly and more importantly, Father said, "Delighted to meet you, my dear. For some time now, I thought I never would. What are we thinking? June? June is a good time for a wedding."

Gerald shook his head. "Father, no. We're getting married in a few weeks."

Father looked between them, made the connection to his wife, and nodded without objection. "Wonderful. When does the announcement go to print?"

"In the morning," Gerald said.

Violet pressed a kiss to her father's cheek and commanded, "Drinks! Victor! It's a celebration, and with Father here we're no longer responsible for Geoffrey."

The door to the parlor opened and Violet spun, expecting to find Hargreaves bringing in coffee or tea, but instead Jack stood there. Mountainous, with broad shoulders and a heavy coat still on. Vi gasped and darted to him, throwing herself into his arms. He staggered back, and she gasped again.

Jack was as strong as an ox and never had he staggered when he caught her. She took his face between her hands and noticed the dark circles under his eyes and a pallor under his tan, and demanded, "What happened?"

"I'm fine," he lied hoarsely. "Everything's fine."

Violet's gaze narrowed on him, and she let go of his cheek to feel his forehead, which was, to her horror, a little warm. It was cold and raining with a chill in the air that could invade your very bones, and Jack was too warm.

"There was a scuff-up," Hamilton said from behind Jack. Violet pulled away from Jack to scowl at Ham. The apology in his expression wasn't enough. "Jack and I were both injured. We lost Hobbs."

Violet gasped, "You lost Hobbs? He's dead?"

Her exclamation had their audience reacting.

"Come and sit, Jack," Father said. "You do look a bit worse for wear."

"He's dead?" Violet repeated in a near-shriek. "Scuffup? Injured how? Victor! Send for our doctor."

"That's not necessary," Jack said mildly while Violet tugged his heavy coat from him. It was only as she removed it that she realized there was a hole in it near the shoulder.

"Is this a bullet hole?" Her horror struck everyone else silent again. "Jack!"

"I'm fine, Violet," he told her gently. "All is well."

"All is not well!"

"It went straight through, missing everything that could cause me trouble. A little time, a little rest, all will be well."

"All is not well," Violet snapped again. She stared at him, her eyes welling with tears, and she didn't know if she was crying out of fury or terror, but she was feeling both.

"Violet," Victor said carefully. "Why don't we let Jack sit?"

"Did you telephone the doctor?" Her anger was sufficient to have Victor holding up both hands.

"I don't need a doctor," Jack said precisely. "I've seen one. I'm patched up. All is well."

Vi turned on him, eyes blazing. She didn't care that all three of her brothers, Lottie, and her father were watching—let alone Ham. "Sit!"

Jack sat, but he grabbed her wrist, pulling her down. He glanced around and then nodded at Lottie, "Jack Wakefield."

"Lottie Wilder," she replied weakly. Her expressive gaze was fixed on him and Violet.

"The doctor," Violet told Victor again.

Jack wrapped his good arm around Violet's shoulder and told her, once again, "I am fine, Violet, and I don't want to bother with a doctor."

Vi turned blazing eyes on him and hissed, "If you expect a single moment of rest or coddling, you are going to see a doctor I trust."

"Vi—" Jack's exhaustion filled her with temporary regret, but it didn't last longer than a moment.

"Vi—" Hamilton's hushed voice was careful as he said, "Violet, I swear to you, Jack saw a very good doctor. It was one of the fellows who took care of us during the war."

"The war!" Violet turned on Ham and Jack's grip on her shoulder went from comforting to constricting.

"Violet," Jack snapped. "I am fine."

She turned back to him, and this time she let him see how she felt. The worry that had been bubbling for days filled her gaze, and he winced.

"Fine. A doctor." He ignored their watching family, tugging her neck towards him and pressing a kiss on her forehead. "If it will make you feel better."

Letting her feelings loose made the stiff upper lip impossible. She pressed her face into his chin to hide the welling of tears until Victor pressed a handkerchief in her hand. It took her long, long minutes to recover herself and when she did, everyone but Victor and Ham had left.

"Are you really all right?" Violet asked Jack.

"I swear to you, Vi. I am."

Violet pulled away from him and then peeked into his suit coat and saw the bulky binding beneath his shirt. She took in a deep breath, let it out slowly, and told him with clear precision, "If you die because of your work, I will desecrate your grave, tell our children horrible stories about you, and use your name as an expletive."

Victor laughed and then snapped his mouth closed when Violet and Jack looked his way. He was saved by the doctor's arrival, who changed Jack's bandages, promised Violet things looked good, and left when Vi started crying again.

CHAPTER 17

The comforting thump of Jack's heartbeat filled Violet's ear the whole of the night. For once, it was her who stayed up late, watching over him. Often, it was Violet's state of mind that left him watching over her. She rubbed his hand while he slept and when his eyes opened, filled with pain, she handed him pills and didn't relax until he swallowed them.

His gaze fixed on hers in the gloom as he settled back into his pillows.

"I'm all right, Vi."

Violet nodded, biting her bottom lip. "I know."

He held back a groan as he adjusted his shoulders. "I didn't mean to scare you."

Vi leaned forward and brushed back his hair. "Did you get him?"

"He can't hurt anyone anymore."

Violet nodded, biting down on her lip harder to hold back her reaction. She didn't want to do anything that added to what he was feeling even though she could see that fighting her emotions bothered him just as much. "I don't know how to feel about any of this."

Jack hooked her neck, pulling her down to lay on his good side. He couldn't make her feel better about the overt example of his mortality, but the kiss that he pressed to her palm and the way he turned her hand, placing it over his heart, helped.

His heart beat under her palm, and she lay in bed thinking. When she was sure he was well asleep, Violet slipped away. She went down to the parlor, dragging the chalkboard back into the parlor with her, lit the lights, and stared. There was nothing more to be seen there, she thought. She had to wonder just what could be found if they could see inside the Kennington brothers' accounts.

Violet paced as she determinedly fixed her mind on the brothers and not on Jack. After a while Ham entered the parlor, followed by Victor. It was quite late, but she wasn't surprised neither of them were asleep.

"Is Jack sleeping?"

Violet nodded.

"What's all this?" Ham asked.

Violet knew her anger with Ham was unfair, but it didn't change the fury that was riding her. She closed her eyes. "I don't like you very much right now, Ham."

"You'll like me less," he replied, "when you realized Jack was shot in the shoulder so I wasn't shot in the heart."

Vi paused in her pacing and ground out. "Are you all right?"

Victor's laugh made Violet turn her furious gaze to him.

"Father went into the library when you took Jack upstairs to be checked out," Victor said, changing the subject. "He talked to Ham and I a while about Geoffrey. The reality of it is—if you've never met Mitchell Fitzhugh, no one should know of his existence or the possibility of him and Eleanor having once been in love. Father also pointed out that Norman Kennington was in Danvers's pocket."

Violet, Ham, and Victor started when the window to the parlor opened.

"Violet, get back," Ham ordered.

A golden angel's head tucked in through the window and Smith grinned engagingly at the people in the room. "Violet," he said, making her gaze narrow darkly on him, "the man who's watching your house isn't worth the money."

"That's Mrs. Wakefield," Ham said with a scowl. "Bloody hell man, couldn't you just tell her that her guard could be better?"

"She also needs updated locks. I'd have thought you'd have taken care of that before now. What did you do? Tell the servants to do it?"

Violet stared at him and then shook her head. She turned back to Ham and Victor and told them, "I can't handle him right now."

"Beatrice lives here, you know," Smith said soberly. "I worry."

Violet stared at him. "She's not your…"

Smith stared at Violet and then lifted a brow.

"Oh!" Violet looked at Victor, unsettled. "I think you should make him go away."

"I'm pretty sure he could kill me with one hand tied

behind his back," Victor told her. "This is no Algernon we're dealing with here. He let himself into and out of a prison. I'm out of my league, darling."

Violet stared and then stalked out of the parlor and up to Beatrice's bedroom at the back of the house. She knocked on the door. Beatrice staggered to the door. She stared at Violet with blinking eyes. "Violet?"

Vi grinned at the use of her first name but it didn't last. "Smith is here. He broke into the house. His justification is that you're here. Honestly, Beatrice darling, you're the only person who can handle him. Would you mind?"

"Does he realize it's 3:00 a.m.?"

"As far as I can tell, he just doesn't care, darling, sweet, wonderful Beatrice. Help me?"

She nodded and stepped back into her room. A moment later, she returned dressed in a simple skirt and jumper. She was also wearing stockings and shoes. The two of them returned to the parlor to find the three men and Jack examining the letters and new paperwork Violet hadn't seen yet.

Smith looked up and shot Violet a dark look, but she barely noted it when she saw Jack sitting with a table in front of him, flipping through paperwork. "Why are you up?"

"You left."

Violet cursed and then laughed when she saw the shock on everyone's face.

"Mr. Wakefield," Beatrice gasped, "are you all right?"

"I'm fine," Jack lied.

Violet looked to Beatrice. "Thank heaven, you're here. The idiocy of mankind is suffocating me."

"Speaking of the idiocy of mankind," Jack told Violet. "Both of the Kenningtons were at the theater tonight?"

Violet nodded.

"And Geoffrey reported that both of them left the theater box," Violet told him. "It would have been easy for one of them to slip the note to Eleanor, but Algie would have been harder. That had to happen while we were in the crowd."

"Maybe they paid an usher to deliver it or something to that effect," Jack suggested. His face was too white for Violet's happiness and she crossed to him, putting her hand against his forehead. He pulled it down to his lips, pressed a kiss on it, and said, "Smith found confirmation that both of the Kennington men have struggled financially since Danvers died. The deconstruction of the Danvers fraud scheme messed with them both."

"But," Violet said, "Markus didn't invest as heavily as Norman, and Markus started out better off."

"Those are both true," Smith said, eyeing Beatrice with a slight frown. What was he thinking, Violet thought, and why was he eyeing Beatrice like that? "Markus could have recovered, but he also lost money gambling and didn't cut back on his spending at all. He could have recovered, but he wasn't smart. Norman was smarter, but he has less to work with."

"Do they have connections to the prison?" Violet asked. "And neither of them would need to visit Harry Mathers to know Lady Eleanor's secrets. How would they know Algie's? We"—Violet gestured to herself and Victor—"didn't know it."

Jack lifted a brow. "You know, we have a unique advantage."

"What's that?" Smith asked.

"Families will forgive each other. Let's have a family dinner, a bit of an intervention, and we could get them to confess."

"No one is going to confess to a murder."

"They don't have to," Jack said exhaustedly. "We'll have them on the murder if we can get them to confess they helped Mathers get out of prison. Favor for an old friend and all that. There's every reason that they might think we'll punish them ourselves and help them save face for the sake of the family."

Violet rubbed her brow and then crossed to Jack, lifting the files from him. "I don't care who murdered Harry Mathers."

"Vi—" Jack took her hand and ran his thumb over her wrist.

"I don't care who is blackmailing my stepmother."

"Vi—" Victor said. "Maybe your middle of the night reasoning isn't how you really feel?"

"Right now," Violet said to Jack, Victor, and beyond them to Ham, Smith, and Beatrice, "the only thing I care about is Jack not losing his rest."

"Victor," Jack said as Violet pulled on his good arm to make him stand, "ask your father to have a family dinner party. The Kenningtons, Gerald and Lottie, Vi and me, you."

"Ham," Violet added.

"I'm not family," Ham said. "If I'm there, they won't talk."

Violet did not agree about him not being family, but she did think he was right. "I wonder if we can make it possible for you to listen. Like we did with Rita's aunt.

You can be there, hear it all, and make sure that it works. Your voice as a witness will carry more weight than anything else."

Ham looked at Jack and back at Violet. "Let's take some time to work out the details. There isn't a rush as long as Lady Eleanor's last blackmail note didn't give her a timeframe."

Jack started to protest, and Violet put her hand over his mouth. "Perfect. Jack, you need rest."

Violet dragged Jack back to bed, glancing with worry at Beatrice.

"She'll be fine," Jack told her. "Ham and Victor will protect her, but she can protect herself. You raised her."

Violet laughed. "She's only a few years younger. Smith, though, who knows how old he is. He'll probably be more and more attractive as he ages."

Jack laughed and then groaned. "Don't leave this time."

"I won't."

"And sleep."

Violet wasn't sure about that, but she fluffed his pillows, got him a glass of water, and then let him pull her into his side. Rather than sleeping on his back, he rolled onto his good side and threw both an arm and a leg over her.

"Doesn't this hurt you?"

"I wasn't sure I'd come back to you, Vi. Holding you helps."

Violet was the one who kissed his hand then. "Jack, I wasn't kidding about desecrating your grave."

"Vi," he replied, "I've talked to Ham. I'm only going to

consult from now on. This is a younger man's game and one who doesn't have what I have."

"So you won't travel anymore?"

"I might travel," he said, "but Ham and I won't be going into the field anymore."

"You're an expert," she said quietly, "you have something to give that others don't."

"They can't have my life. Not when I have you," he said, holding her tighter.

She shuddered in relief and asked, "Will Ham's superiors let him stop going into the field?"

"They didn't love he went to Leeds, Vi. Ham will be fine."

Violet heard Jack slide into sleep as his breathing deepened and slowed. Was Jack leaving Scotland Yard because of her? She knew that he was, but was she selfish to let him? Would consulting and advising other detectives be enough for him? And if it wasn't, what could he do that wouldn't put him at risk?

Violet worried about it until sleep overtook her and for once Jack slept in, so they made it well into the next day before either of them shifted.

CHAPTER 18

*M*arkus and Norman Kennington were as handsome as Lady Eleanor was lovely, Violet thought as she greeted both of her stepmother's brothers, as did Gerald and Lottie. It was Lottie's first family dinner, and Violet didn't think that it was a good introduction to the larger family, but Gerald said Lottie should know what she was getting into.

"How are you feeling, Jack?" the earl asked as he shook Jack's hand.

"Better," Jack answered.

They accepted cocktails from Victor who had taken over at the bar, and Violet watched as they all smiled, chatting about the weather and children in school. The days following Jack's return had only cemented Eleanor's brothers, or at least one of them, as her blackmailer as they turned over each other possibility. Violet watched them both carefully and was surprised that the hatred in their gazes as they looked at Eleanor didn't set the room on fire.

Over the first course, Violet watched her father smoothly interact with his brothers-in-law and realized that he lied with aplomb and an ease that Violet could only envy. She sat at Jack's right at equal distance from both ends of the table. In these surrounds, she and Jack were of the least importance. Violet glanced at him, noting the healthy color of his skin, the brightness in his eyes, the way he took his wine glass without a wince, and let herself relax.

Soup, fish, vegetables. All excellently done with a determination, Violet thought, to showcase the richness of the Carlyle house despite it being a family dinner. Everyone but Lottie seemed to treat the meal as though they feasted as such every day. Though it was apparent that Wanda Kennington, Markus's wife, enjoyed the dinner. She let the bites savor in her mouth. Violet hated the way she was about to ruin it.

"Wanda," Violet asked, "is it true that you lost a thousand pounds in whist?"

She gasped and paled, glancing at her husband before her gaze turned to her plate.

"By Jove, Carlyle, what's wrong with your daughter?" Markus's rage was palpable, and Violet was grateful for Jack's comforting hand. "Why would she say such nonsense?"

"Her man of business uncovered it," the earl replied calmly as though such a loss were commonplace. "That and her private investigator. Did you know? Violet and Jack have been known to employ a rather singular gentleman named Smith. I don't think that can be his real name, can it Vi?"

"I don't believe so," Vi said merrily despite the way her stomach roiled at the sight of Wanda's distress. Violet turned to her twin who looked as sick as she felt. "Victor?"

"Oh, I imagine not. I've always assumed that he is the perpetrator of some terrible crime and on the run."

Markus was sputtering at this point, and Norman had a smirk on his face that was as cruel as his wife's. They watched Wanda as she attempted to rally.

"But it's Norman who really is interesting," Victor said with a relish that counteracted their uncle's smirk. "Losing much of your fortune to Danvers's crimes. Speculating more wildly and losing the rest. How long have you been living on nothing?"

Lady Eleanor's mouth had dropped open in realization and her cold hiss made even Violet shiver. "It's you, isn't it? Who else would know—" Her voice cut off as Norman turned on her.

"About what? The cuckoo? The way you throw Carlyle's name around like your personal shield? Did you know Geoffrey and Isolde aren't yours, Carlyle?"

Violet flinched at Isolde's name, but her father didn't blink. "Of course they are mine."

"You clearly haven't met Mitchell Fitzhugh. Geoffrey is a spitting image. And Isolde—"

"Isolde, like Violet," her father cut in, "has my mother's jawline. If you'll take careful note, you'd see that the twins and Isolde both have the same shape of eyes."

"And Geoffrey?" Norman shot back. "You've had

another man's chick in your nest, draining your finances, eating your food, being dressed by your coin. Fool."

"Geoffrey looks exactly like my uncle," Violet's father lied. His smile was even and his laugh was entirely undisturbed. "I can show you a painting sometime if you'd like."

The two brothers met each other's gazes and burst into mocking laughter while Eleanor glared daggers at them both.

"You turn on each other so quickly," Jack said as though he were watching mold grow. "I'm an only child myself, but I have to wonder if all siblings are like this. I assume that Victor and Violet's devotion is unique as twins."

Both of the Kennington men looked at Jack as though he were the fool and Violet's gaze narrowed on them.

"Why are you having us investigated, Violet? Why are you paying your men to lie?" Markus Kennington demanded, jowls flapping with his anger.

"My stepmother is being blackmailed."

Those beady, cold eyes narrowed on Violet and he snapped, "Everyone knows you hate her. She's certainly listed your many ill qualities at our table many a time. Why bother helping her?" It was telling that he took the news of blackmail without comment.

"In my opinion, it's what families do. Even when there are harsher feelings between us, we rally round."

His laughter told her what they thought of her naïveté. She looked at Jack, who said clearly, "We know it was you who was blackmailing your sister." He purposefully did not let his gaze settle on either brother.

The two brothers glanced at each other. Violet waited with her breath held. Would they turn on one another?

Then Markus asked Norman, "Is that how you paid me? With money you clawed out of Eleanor?"

Norman glared at Markus and the two brothers were shooting looks back and forth that were so deadly, Violet felt certain one would be felled before long.

"We also know," Jack said, "that it was you who was visiting with Mathers in the prison, Markus."

Markus choked and his wife gasped, "Markus? No. No, not you."

He growled at her. "What was I to do, Wanda, with all your debts?"

Her gaze darted back to her plate, but this time a tear fell. Violet dug her fingernails into Jack's wrist as the shooting accusations exploded into unintelligible shouting between the brothers, Eleanor, and Norman's wife.

After long minutes, Father roared, "Enough!"

The command was enough to silence the room. Father rose and glanced down the table. "Let me be clear about what we know."

The two brothers eyed the earl as if he were a serpent about to strike.

"You were both blackmailing Eleanor."

When the protests started, Violet's father held up a silencing hand.

"Do me the courtesy of not lying to me when we all know the truth. We're family, are we not?"

Violet noted the gleam of relief in Norman's gaze, but Markus's guard didn't fade. His wife was biting her lip, gaze on her plate, while Norman's wife was leaned back watching like a cat who saw a canary. They were, Violet thought, disgusting with their masks removed.

"You should have done a better job of hiding your deposits, Markus. They match what Eleanor paid." Jack's voice was low and threatening.

The two brothers eyed each other and then Norman turned away. "You have so much," he accused the earl.

Violet bit down on her lip to keep from speaking. She might have started the battle, but she knew that they'd be far more likely to give the information that her father wanted if she said nothing. She was also quite taken aback that her stepmother hadn't spoken up. Instead, Lady Eleanor was sitting still and silent, watching the event unfold with pursed lips and narrowed eyes.

"Eleanor never has to pay for what she's done," Markus said. "Why is it only us who suffer?"

Wanda started and Violet realized that she at least had no idea. Adele, however, had known. Violet threaded her fingers through Jack's as Eleanor cursed both of her brothers.

"You were the one who dragged us into Danvers's plot," Markus accused his sister.

Her gaze narrowed as she hissed, "But that's not true. Danvers approached me because he wanted Isolde. He knew things that—" Her gaze darted to her husband and a light flush crossed her cheeks.

"He knew that Isolde and Geoffrey weren't Carlyle's," Markus finished for her with a curled lip.

"Leave my children out of it, Kennington," Violet's father said in a silky, cold threat. "Leave them out of it or things change."

"Don't be stupid, Carlyle," Markus shot back but

backed down when the earl glared at him. The expression on his face was murderous. Markus held up both hands as he muttered, "Or be stupid. Whatever you want, my lord."

"The blackmail stops now," the earl commanded. His steely gaze hit each brother, and Violet wondered if they thought they'd actually gotten away with murder given the fake apology on their faces.

"Of Algernon as well," Victor said low and even. Violet shivered as her beloved brother sounded just as threatening.

"What are you talking about?" Markus demanded. He wasn't pretending. His beady gaze turned to Norman, who smirked.

"I needed money more than you did."

"But Algie didn't pay," Victor said, watching the two brothers. Norman grimaced with one abrupt nod. Markus eyed his brother smugly.

The only question left was if both or just one had murdered Harry Mathers. "Is that why you tried to see if Danvers had been blackmailing anyone else?" Victor asked Norman.

"Should have known Danvers didn't have anything," Norman said snidely. "We gave him Eleanor before his idiot son killed him."

"So you took Algie Allyn for yourself?" Markus demanded.

"You're the one who spent too much money getting Mathers out of jail on the off-chance that his fairytale blackmail book was the real thing," Norman shot back. "Idiot."

Markus didn't deny it, and Violet turned to look at her father who had been carefully taking all this in.

"So it was you who visited the jail? Bribed the guards?" the earl asked evenly as though it weren't part one of a murder confession.

"Norman suggested that Danvers might have been blackmailing more than just Eleanor. It was stupid. We can fix this, Henry," Markus said. There was a bargaining in his voice as he addressed Violet's father. "We can fix this and make it right again."

"We could fix it," the earl agreed quietly. "What's a little blackmail between siblings? Did you go to the prison too, Norman?"

Norman shook his head. "Markus's plan made me think, but Mathers? That man is clever. If he has something that could help him get out of prison, he'd have used it before Markus showed up."

Violet noted the present tense and so did her father. His gaze landed for a long time on Norman, considering.

The earl looked at his wife and then back to her brothers. "I wasn't a very good husband for a while there. You blackmailed your sister because I let things fall apart between us, and Ellie didn't feel like she could turn to me. That's not all right with me."

"She'll be affected by this if you let it get out," Markus said with a grin. "People will wonder why she could be blackmailed. Rumors will abound. Better to keep this between the family walls, so to speak."

The earl steepled his fingers. His gaze traveled around the table. From Markus and the upset Wanda, to Gerald and Lottie, the countess, the twins and Jack, Adele and Norman.

"It amazes me that three siblings raised together can hate each other so much when I have raised my own separately who support and protect each other. Why is it, I wonder? I'd guess bad blood, but Isolde and Geoffrey carry your blood, and they aren't arguing rats."

Violet winced at the chill in her father's voice.

"You've found us out," Markus said without remorse. "A new game will have to be afoot."

"It was a safe crime," Norman agreed. "No one turns in a sibling for blackmail. We'd all be tarnished by the same brush."

The cheerfulness in his voice made Violet want to sick up. It was a safe bet that he'd get away with what they'd done to their own sister.

"For blackmail, you're right," the earl agreed. "And as you said, my family won't be ruined by the loss of whatever Eleanor sold to pay the two of you." The earl paused. "Murder, however, is another story."

CHAPTER 19

"Murder?" Lady Eleanor demanded.

"Murder," Wanda echoed. Somehow, she didn't seem all that surprised. Violet had to wonder if they should have talked to Wanda from the beginning.

"What nonsense is this?" Markus demanded. "No one died."

"Mathers did," Jack said.

"Mathers escaped," Norman argued. "Not that I helped with that. It was all Markus."

Violet shook her head and tucked herself closer to Jack. The quick abandoning of Markus shocked her, though it shouldn't have given the Kennington family and their lack of love for one another.

"This was your idea," Markus said to Norman. "And now you're trying to say that you didn't have anything to do with it?"

"I didn't have anything to do with Mathers. I told you

that was a loss from the beginning. Did you really kill him?" The exclamation was out and out gleeful.

"Of course I didn't. Mathers escaped."

"Mathers thought he was escaping," Jack countered. "He didn't survive the night."

"I don't know what you're talking about."

"You can't honestly believe you weren't revealed? What would the guard have to gain by keeping your name out when confronted?" Jack challenged, though no one had confronted a guard that couldn't be found.

However, Markus was suddenly uncertain.

"The only reason you have tonight is to convince the earl to help you," Jack continued. "Give him a reason."

Markus stared at the earl who returned the look starkly. The cold hatred on her father's face made Violet shiver, and Jack wrapped his arm around her. At the same time, Victor reached out and took her hand. The earl might despise his brother-in-law, but Violet, Victor, and Gerald—along with Isolde and Geoffrey—would never have reason to feel the same about theirs. They had chosen too well.

"Henry—" Markus pled. "Henry, I was ruined."

"So you killed him?"

"He said he would tell Eleanor. That he'd write to her if I didn't get him out of jail. I—I couldn't risk him doing to me what—"

"What you were doing to my wife?"

Markus looked frantically around the table. "He'd have hurt us all!"

"He hadn't yet," Violet finally said. "He had been in jail for years and he'd never revealed what he knew about Eleanor. He wasn't that kind of man."

"He was a liar and a thief who helped Danvers steal our money," Markus spewed furiously. "Your husband made sure he paid for what he did. How long did it take to put him in jail, Jack? Nearly a year?"

Violet looked at her husband, saw his flexing jaw, and knew that his own fury was held back only by his respect for her father. This was the earl's table, his house, and—to be fair—his mess.

The earl did not, however, have anything else to discover. "Detective Barnes?" he called. "I think that's enough."

A moment later the door the servants used opened and Ham stepped into the dining room with a uniformed constable. "It's enough."

Markus leapt to his feet cursing just as his wife crumpled to the floor. He didn't even hesitate as he rushed over her for the dining room door. Lady Eleanor screamed and pretended to faint while the constable waiting in the hall caught her brother.

Violet left the room while Markus Kennington was tackled and taken away. Eleanor and Adele were screaming at each other and only Lottie bothered to look after Wanda.

Violet squeezed Jack's hand and made her way up the stairs to her brother Geoffrey.

"Is it over?" Geoffrey asked as he stood.

Violet nodded and crossed to him. She wrapped her arms around his waist and told him, "It's all right, Geoffrey."

"It'll out. Sooner or later."

"It won't matter as long as Father acts like people are idiots and the rest of us treat you the same as always."

Geoffrey was stiff next to Violet, a stone-framed body. She could guess at his worries. "You know that we love Ginny."

He nodded.

"Who contributed to her, and your, making matters so much less than who loved you and cared for you through your lives."

Geoffrey nodded and then he looked at her. "Why do you care about me, Vi?"

"You're my brother."

"We weren't raised together. We aren't really related. Why do you care?"

Violet squeezed him again. "You were always mine. Just like Isolde."

Geoffrey sniffed, holding back his emotions, winning at the stiff upper lip while Violet failed. "Isolde is your sister, though."

"Is she? Markus said she wasn't."

"Markus is wrong," Geoffrey muttered. "You do have the look of each other at times, Vi. What will happen to him?"

Violet shrugged. "He was arrested. Ham will let Norman go because Father and Lady Eleanor won't want to pursue anything. Markus? There's no body, Geoffrey. If Markus is very clever, he could get away with his crimes. If he isn't? He's going to prison for a good long while. I fear, either way, it will be a long battle."

"I wish I wasn't related to him. I feel...dirty."

Violet shook her head fiercely. "Family is what you make of it, Geoffrey. You, Ginny, me, Jack. None of us share blood, but we're all family. Markus shares some of your blood, but he isn't family. Not like he should have been."

～

VIOLET STAYED with Geoffrey until Jack and her father came to fetch them.

"Son?" the earl said to Geoffrey and held out a hand. "Come, join Gerald, Victor, and I. I have decided a walk is in order. I have need of my boys."

Geoffrey rose slowly. The room was tense, and the feelings were as vibrant in the moment as the ones Violet had experienced earlier at dinner. Only with the Kennington siblings, the emotion had been hatred and jealousy. With the Carlyle siblings, it was acceptance and love. The earl waited until Geoffrey was close, drew him in, and hugged him tightly. Whatever he whispered had Geoffrey's shoulders shuddering and Violet cried along with her father as they both wiped away a tear. They'd escaped the shadows of the past and stepped into the light of their own making.

It was enough.

The END

Hullo friends! I am so grateful you dove in for the next Violet Carlyle mystery. I hope you've enjoyed this book. If you wouldn't mind, I would be so grateful for a review.

. . .

THE SEQUEL to this book is available now.

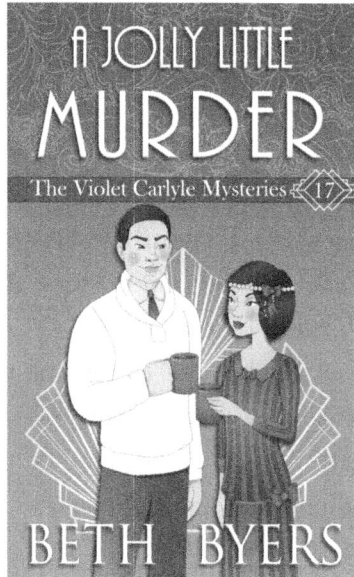

December 1925

Violet Wakefield is determined to dive into the holiday and enjoy every occasion. She's going to see the live nativity, listen to Handel's Messiah, and attend the Nutcracker ballet. She'll cover her house in all the holly and lights. In fact, Vi wants nothing more than to put up the largest Christmas tree she can locate and stuff it with gifts.

She little expects, however, to stumble across a crime in action. When she gets pulled into the madness, her biggest concern isn't the crime, it's keeping Jack from committing a holiday homicide.

Order Your Copy Here.

A new historical mystery series is now available.

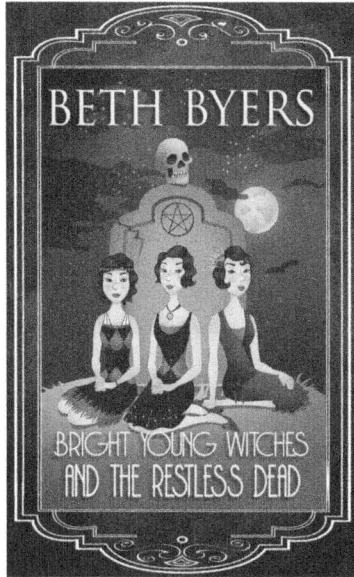

April 1922

When the Ku Klux Klan appears at the door of the Wode sisters, they decide it's time to visit the ancestral home in England.

With squabbling between the sisters, it takes them too long to realize that their new friend is being haunted. Now they'll have to set aside their fight, discover just why their friend is being haunted, and what they're going to do about it. Will they rid their friend of the ghost and out themselves as witches? Or will they look away?

Join the Wodes as they rise up and embrace just who and what they are in this newest historical mystery adventure.

Order your copy here. Or keep scrolling for a sneak peek of the first chapter.

SNEAK PEEK OF THE BRIGHT YOUNG & THE RESTLESS DEAD

CHAPTER ONE

APRIL 1922. WASHINGTON D.C. USA

ARIADNE EUDORA WISTERIA WODE

"Give me some of the good stuff," the man said, nudging a waiting girl aside. He was wearing a pinstriped evening suit with his hair pomaded back. Given the large ring on his pinky and the gold on his watch chain, Ariadne assumed he was quite wealthy or quite powerful or both. The large cigar hanging from his mouth suggested both.

Ariadne had been just behind him when he went shoving people about and she caught the girl he'd sent stumbling off her bar stool. The height of the girl's heels didn't help, but the man hadn't even noticed he'd knocked the woman down. The girl shot him a nasty, unnoticed look and then turned to Ariadne with a glance that said, Can you believe this dirty bloke?

"We're out," the barman said. "Want a Coke?"

The shelves behind him were nearly empty of bottles, unlike the bar itself, which was full. Ariadne sighed. The speakeasy never ordered enough, always ran low, and then the boss took it out on her. He needed either more suppliers, to quit under-ordering, or to open a little less often. Some of the fellows in the bar were reeling drunk and could have been cut off before they'd reached that state. Sloppy drunks put everyone at risk of getting pinched.

"Give me what the management is drinking," the man growled. "I know you got the good stuff, and I don't want any of this second-rate swill that'll leave me blind or dead."

"Our delivery of the good stuff is late," the barman said flatly. Whoever this shove-y man was, the barman was unimpressed. "No one's drinking much until that comes along. Not even the boss man."

Ariadne met the barman's gaze, and he jerked his head to the back. There was a triggerman guarding the door, and the man didn't move when Ariadne approached. His dark eyes fixed on hers, and there was threat in his stony expression.

Here we go again, Ariadne thought, ignoring his look and sliding past him without a flicker of a lash. Posturing was such a gent's move. She had too much to do for this nonsense. When she felt someone watching her, she glanced back and caught the gaze of a bloke with dark, sharp eyes and slicked back hair, with a hefty drink in front of him. He was, she thought, almost certainly a copper. Hopefully he was dirty. Otherwise, they'd all be hauled away with time in the slammer. The goons anyway. The shadows liked Ariadne.

Either way, she wished she was a little less memorable in the drop-waisted, shimmery dress that showed off far more of her chest than she'd prefer. She dressed with the intent to blend in with the other dames. Better to be seen as an easy moll than what she was—a lady-legger. Or, more accurately, a booze-making witch.

"It's about time," Blind Bobby growled as Ariadne appeared. "Do you have it? I don't pay full price for late goods. You're costing me a pile of lettuce, girl."

"They had checkpoints on the way in. I had to think quick and step even more quickly. You're lucky I'm here at all, and you'll be paying me the full amount or I'll take a walk down to the next juice joint. Easy peasy." She snapped her fingers. It was always better not to be too challenging, but sometimes she couldn't help herself.

Blind Bobby put his gun on the table and leaned back. "Maybe I'll just take the booze and pay you nothing, little girl."

"Did you find someone else who makes gin that won't blind you and can age wine and whisky with magic— because I don't think you have found anyone like me."

"I'll pay you eighty percent." He sniffed and growled, "From here on."

His dark, beady eyes fixed on her, and he leaned in, strong jaw gritted. He intended to scare her, but Ariadne was only irritated. She felt as though every time she interacted with this grunting beast, he thought he could just tower over her face and she'd crumple. Ariadne laughed, a trilling thing that didn't sound amused but conveyed her message.

Blind Billy nudged his gun once again, and Ariadne scowled at him, dropping all pretense of amusement. She crossed her arms over her chest and lifted a challenging brow instead. "Do you really want to put a bean shooter up against magic?"

"Do you really want to put you and your little sister against my boys? There's even smaller witch brats in that town of yours. What's it called? Nighton? Bring her in." The last was said to one of the apes standing about grasping their guns trying to look intimidating.

There was a sound at the tunnel door and several men poured through with Ariadne's sister, Echo. She struggled in the grasp of...Ariadne's head cocked and gaze narrowed.

Lindsey Noel. She scowled at him. He was the shining son of Nighton and the fellow intent on finding his way into Ariadne's sister Circe's knickers.

"Well, if it isn't Lindsey Noel. Are you joining in on threatening my sisters? All of my sisters?"

Lindsey blushed, but his voice was mean. "I know where you live." His fingers dug into Echo's bicep.

"And I know where you live." Ariadne glanced at Echo, who seemed fine despite the white circles under Lindsey's pressing fingers. "Why'd you let them take you?"

"I wanted to see what Lindsey was up to. Sooner or later, Circe will see he's milquetoast playing at being a leading man. She believes that front he puts up, but the mannered handsome puppy will fade into what he really is—another arrogant rube with a rich daddy. It'll go easier if it's me telling her what he did, and after all—he put his hands on me."

Easier, Ariadne translated, than if Ari were the one who told Circe her lover put them all at risk with his playing at being a bad boy.

The idiot Lindsey let go of Echo, but it was too late. The smirk she shot him was enough to have him wondering, would he lose Circe over this? The unfortunate answer was that Ariadne could only wish.

The other men glanced at each other, smirking, when Blind Billy grunted, "No one cares about your hick problems." He gestured and the goons lining the wall leveled their guns at Ariadne.

She sighed. "Until I get paid, you won't be able to open the bottles at the delivery point. Try as you might."

Blind Bobby laughed meanly and Ariadne yawned. He shoved the table back, grabbing his gun as he did, and shoved it into Ariadne's face, pressing it hard against her forehead.

"Careful," she said quietly, "guns do malfunction so easily."

"Open the whiskey, Petey," Blind Billy ordered.

Ariadne rolled her eyes and telepathically told her sister, Draw your magic. Ariadne opened her mind and senses to her own magic. She'd originally approached Blind Billy once prohibition went into effect because the church basement where the speakeasy was housed was a place of power. Her magic, always strong, thrummed through her with a vengeance here. Echo's must be a tsunami of power given the dead that even Ariadne could sense.

The ghosts are restless, Echo sent.

175

Of course they are, it's a desecrated church. How did Noel know about us?

Echo's mental snort seemed to ricochet about Ariadne's head and they both knew the answer: Circe. Soft, trusting, blind-with-love Circe. Lindsey Noel wasn't surprised in the least by their magic. Their sister hated keeping what they were from her 'sweet' Lindsey. She must have talked, and he'd gathered a full confession, given his presence.

Foolish girl.

The grunting of his man trying to open the bottle caught her attention. The goon was yanking at the stopper in the whiskey bottle, desperate to open it. He finally brought out a large knife, but it bounded off of the glass as though it were stone instead of a little bit of cork and glass. Finally he looked up at Blind Billy and shook his head.

Blind Billy pulled the gun back enough just to shove it back against her head again. "That's gonna leave a bruise." His laugh was ugly and he glanced at his men until they were snorting with unbelievable laughter as well.

"Balm of Gilead is an easy enough potion to make for someone like me," Ariadne told him, drawing her magic so deeply that her bobbed hair was slowly starting to rise around her face. "The bruise will be gone in minutes. I carry it in my handbag."

"What about the hole my bullet leaves?" He cocked his gun and then, to her horror, swung his arm wide, aiming at Echo. "Will it cure that?"

"Fool," Ariadne said, finished with this nonsense. She dropped to her knees, covering her head when the gun misfired, and magic rushed into Ariadne as the place of power energized her and she sent the rest of the guns into either misfiring or not firing at all.

With Echo there, ghosts were caught in the energy in the church and within the sisters. The ghosts went mad, merging into a tornado of shadows that sent Blind Billy's goons into shrieking like little girls. Point of fact, Ariadne thought as she started to crawl away from Blind Billy, her little sisters wouldn't have whined like these boys.

A moment later, the copper from earlier rushed the door. Ariadne dropped her magic immediately so it seemed that the screaming goons had gone crazy. On her knees, with forced tears, she looked like a victim as she reached for the copper. She screamed to draw his attention to her from Echo. "Help! Help me, please!"

Police swarmed the room, and Ariadne was yanked to her feet by the first copper to reach her. He glanced her over, muttered, "Fool doll," and shoved her behind him.

She shivered and whimpered and thanked the whole of the group repetitively with big crocodile tears, backing towards the wall. Her dress, her mussed makeup, and her tears were enough for the blokes to not realize she was one of the criminals. Just another doll caught up with the wrong man. She waited until they were all looking the other way, wrestling the goons down, and she slid into the shadows, pulling them around her.

The coppers didn't know about the escape tunnel where Echo had already disappeared, followed by Lindsey Noel. Echo had sealed it against any but Ariadne, so the fuzz were gathering up the men who couldn't use their tunnel while she slipped through, cloaked in darkness and magic.

Using the athamé in her handbag, Ariadne carved a rune of the door to keep it locked. She ignored the skittering of rats and the cool touch of the dead as she hurried down the tunnel.

"Go back to sleep," she murmured to the dead, hoping they'd comply. Otherwise the boys who worked for Blind Billy would find themselves chilled in body and spirit.

The old church had a crypt underneath, so it was better not to look into the dark entrances of side rooms if you wanted to avoid looking at the remnants of the living. The tunnels went from the crypt to beyond the graveyard behind the church, following beneath the road. Blind Billy's men had extended the tunnels even farther. With that kind of work ethic, what might those goons have been capable of if they bothered working for good?

Ariadne mocked herself—knowing she was a criminal too—and moved quickly through the tunnels. There were exits for a good mile down the tunnel road if you knew where to look and what to look for.

The vast majority of Ariadne's booze delivery was still in the auto garage where one of the exits from the tunnels led. The bottles were loaded on the back of her truck. Echo already had their truck running and was just loading the last of the whiskey bottles that had been previously unloaded. Any speakeasy could make gin in their bathtub. Magically aged liqueurs, wines, and whiskey required a witch, a different country, or a very expensive operation that risked prison time. Ariadne sealed the tunnel behind her with the same rune she'd used before. Someone would have to find the runes she'd used and destroy them before the exit would open. Otherwise it would take hours for the spell to fade.

She looked away from her spell and eyed her sister. Echo looked a little mussed but none the worse for wear. "Anyone left here?"

"Just Timmy," Echo grunted as she grabbed the bag of their clothes from behind the truck's seat. "Poor boy. My spell got him hard in the gut when he tried to dodge. He'll have sore ribs if Blind Billy doesn't kill him for losing us and the booze."

"Did Lindsey get out?" Ariadne asked as she shimmied out of her evening gown. Echo tossed Ariadne a wool skirt and blouse, and they stripped down in the auto garage, changing from party clothes to one step away from an initiate for a nunnery.

"He got out when I did, but he was bright enough not to follow me here. We need to consider a change of employment. If things had gone differently, Circe would be raising Medea and Cassiopeia. I love Circe, but..."

Ariadne winced. It was true. If there had been more coppers or if the fellows were a little more trigger happy, they'd have been in trouble. With enough guns blazing, even witches wouldn't have survived.

Ariadne told Echo, "Aunt Beatrix said she was interested in taking over. She has more people. That...that... flimflam that just happened to us wouldn't have happened to her. Not with her sons. Jasper and Gerard with those broad shoulders and thick jaws? Let alone their magic? They won't get the same garbage we're getting."

"We'll still get our cut too," Echo reminded Ariadne with a telling glance. "Beatrix promised it when she wanted to take on the work. You engineered the spells for aging the booze like we do, and Beatrix knows it. We have to be careful, Ariadne—at least until Medea and Cassiopeia are older. They're too little to lose you too."

It wasn't Echo's words that convinced Ariadne. It was the memory of the gun being swung her sister's way. If Echo hadn't been prepared for someone to turn their gun on her, if her magic hadn't been inclined towards the dead, if they'd been firing guns haphazardly, if the sisters had been a little less lucky, Ariadne might have lost her sister. No amount of dough was worth that.

IF YOU ENJOYED THIS SAMPLE, the rest of the book can be found by clicking here.

ALSO BY BETH BYERS

The Violet Carlyle Cozy Historical Mysteries

Murder & the Heir

Murder at Kennington House

Murder at the Folly

A Merry Little Murder

New Year's Madness: A Short Story Anthology

Valentine's Madness: A Short Story Anthology

Murder Among the Roses

Murder in the Shallows

Gin & Murder

Obsidian Murder

Murder at the Ladies Club

Weddings Vows & Murder

A Jazzy Little Murder

Murder by Chocolate

A Friendly Little Murder

Murder by the Sea

Murder On All Hallows

Murder in the Shadows

A Jolly Little Murder

Hijinks & Murder

Love & Murder

A Zestful Little Murder (coming soon)

A Murder Most Odd (coming soon)

Nearly A Murder (coming soon)

The Poison Ink Mysteries

Death By the Book

Death Witnessed

Death by Blackmail

Death Misconstrued

Deathly Ever After

Death in the Mirror

A Merry Little Death

Death Between the Pages (coming soon)

The Hettie and Ro Adventures

co-written with Bettie Jane

Philanderers Gone

Adventurer Gone

Holiday Gone

Aeronaut Gone

The 2nd Chance Diner Mysteries

Spaghetti, Meatballs, & Murder

Cookies & Catastrophe

Poison & Pie

Double Mocha Murder

Made in the USA
Coppell, TX
15 July 2020